"A well-told everyday story that makes wholly satisfying reading . . . because it has real problems, moving episodes, and suspense. Young horse-lovers will like the specific details of horse care."—*The Horn Book*

"The story moves along at an exciting pace that the children will appreciate . . . lovely illustrations are 'a perfect complement to words.'"—*Catholic Library World*

". . . it has excellent developmental values in the boy's relationship with his father and deaf-mute mother and in his understanding and surmounting of his problems with the other boys . . ."—*Library Journal*

"Their adventures keep the story moving at a fast pace but more important is the boy's discovery that his handicap need not keep him from a career of service to others."—Rochester *Democrat & Chronicle*

Also by Marjorie Reynolds

THE CABIN ON GHOSTLY POND

A Horse Called Mystery

A HORSE

CALLED MYSTERY

by MARJORIE REYNOLDS

Pictures by Wesley Dennis

A HARPER TROPHY BOOK

HARPER & ROW, PUBLISHERS
NEW YORK, EVANSTON, SAN FRANCISCO, LONDON

A HORSE CALLED MYSTERY

First published in 1964. 6th printing, 1966.
Large type edition published 1967.

First Harper Trophy Book printing, 1972.

Standard Book Number: 06–440018–2

*For Christopher, Stephanie, Jennifer,
Katrin, Fiona, and Averil*

A Horse Called Mystery

ONE

Owlie gave a hop with his lame leg which brought him up the steps into the school bus. Limping down the aisle, he found an empty seat by an open window, sat down, and settled his books and lunch box on his knees. All around him voices, shrill with excitement at the prospect of summer vacation, called back and forth.

"Come down to the ball field."

"Bring the bat, Mike."

"Doug, lend me your catcher's mitt, will you?"

"I'll meet you at your house, Andy."

Owlie sat quietly. From long experience he had learned that if you are short for your age, have a limp, and wear big round glasses that are always slipping down on your nose, no one wants you on his ball team. He had grown accustomed to standing about while sides were being chosen for games at school until at last someone would say, "Well, I guess we have to take Owlie."

The bus started with a jerk, and the last boy on dropped into the empty seat beside him. It was Roy Bladen, the best ball player in the class, whom Owlie had helped more than once with a math problem.

Owlie smiled with one side of his mouth and glanced in shy friendliness around the corner of his glasses, but Roy was talking to Bud Dover across the aisle so Owlie turned toward the window.

Now the bus was in low gear, climbing up Seacoast Road. Through the open window he could smell the fresh salt breeze blowing off the harbor. Soon they would be passing Westerly, Dr. Delafield's big house on the cliff. It was the finest place anywhere around, and Owlie was very proud that his father was in charge there. The doctor practiced medicine in Chicago and came to Westerly for only two months in the summer.

"Hey, Owlie!" Bud Dover grinned, showing a broken tooth, and his voice sounded unpleasantly from across the aisle over the rattle and clatter of the bus. "Hey, Owlie, I'll bet your father loses his job."

"Why?" asked Owlie, leaning tensely across Roy to stare at Bud.

"You must have read the papers." Bud's voice was full of false innocence. "You know about Dr. Delafield's accident, don't kid me."

"He's not dead," said Owlie stoutly. "He'll come back again someday. Just because he's not coming this summer doesn't mean he won't ever come again."

"Gee, it was terrible," said Bud.

Owlie could have punched him; he didn't sound a bit sorry, only gloating over an exciting newspaper story. "Dr. Delafield was a hero," said Owlie belligerently. "He saved that girl when the hospital burned."

"Yeah, and he went back in again because he was afraid maybe everyone wasn't out," mocked Bud, "and the firemen had to rescue *him*. Pretty dumb, I'd say. Everyone *was* out, and now he's all burned up himself."

"Well, he's not dead," repeated Owlie, who was thrown abruptly back when the bus gave a sudden lurch as it rounded a curve.

By turning his head he could see the great mass of Westerly in the midst of lawns and flower beds. Its many windows had been shuttered and boarded up to protect them during the winter against gales roaring in off the ocean. The house had a desolate

3

appearance as it stood all closed and silent in the calm summer air.

Owlie knew his father's job at Westerly was one of responsibility. The neatly mown lawns, the bright flower beds, where weeds wouldn't dare show their heads for more than half a minute, were all his work. The care of the house, putting up and taking down the shutters, checking the roof for leaks in the winter, painting the boats—all that work was done by him. He could do anything. A "handy man," the doctor often said. Owlie knew he had every reason to be proud of his father.

"Dr. Delafield must be awfully rich." Bud shouted loudly so everyone could hear above the rattle of the bus. "He must be awfully rich to be able to hire your father as a handyman to hang around all year doing nothing."

Owlie could feel the blood of fury rush into his face, and he clenched his fists.

"Shut up, Bud," said Roy. "You're a bully."

The bus was stopping; it was time to get off.

Owlie lived in a small gray cottage at the bottom of a steep lane that ended at a dock which jutted into the harbor. Halfway down the lane lived Bud Dover. Owlie wished that he and Bud didn't get off at the same stop. He remembered too many

4

times when Bud had tripped him on the way home, or taunted him because he was short, or called him four-eyes, or asked him why he didn't walk with one leg on the bank beside the road so he wouldn't limp. To avoid that walk toward home with Bud, Owlie often stopped off at Westerly to talk to his father.

Now as he followed with his limping step Bud's long stride down the aisle, he imagined himself taking a deep breath which would make him grow six feet tall, so that he would be strong enough to knock down his tormentor in the dusty road with one blow on the chin. He took the deep breath but naturally nothing happened, and he found himself out in the sunshine and fresh salty air. The bus was disappearing down the road in the direction of the village, and Bud stood grinning at him with a scornful look on his face.

Owlie edged away and headed toward the gates of Westerly, determined not to walk along the lane until Bud had vanished inside his own door.

"What's the matter? Aren't you going home?" called Bud.

"Later," said Owlie, "I have to speak to Dad."

He followed the drive of crushed clamshells which gleamed white in the sun, and as he walked he looked ahead at the big house whose shuttered windows gave it a blank and lonesome appearance. By now, in other years, Dr. Delafield would have been expected. Every window would have been open, airing the musty smell of winter out of the closed rooms.

The doctor's wife had died a few years before, and as he found it lonely in the big house without her, he frequently asked people to visit him during the summer. Often the guests he invited turned out to be in need of a rest and fresh air, people who perhaps wouldn't have been able to afford a vacation at the seashore without an invitation from the doctor.

Owlie passed in front of the house and twanged the rope of a white metal flagpole standing in the midst of blue hydrangea bushes. He looked far up to the brass ball on top and remembered that when Dr. Delafield was in residence, the Stars and Stripes was run up every morning by his father and lowered every evening at sundown by the doctor himself.

Walking across the lawn to the cliff's edge, Owlie looked down the steep wooden steps leading to a strip of white beach below. Ripples ran ashore, and out beyond in the harbor a sailboat was moving slowly in the light breeze. He watched her come into the wind, sails shaking, then heel over on the port tack and set off merrily across the sun-spangled water.

His glance lingered on an island lying about three hundred yards off shore. Everyone in the village understood that this island was private property belonging to the doctor, and they would as soon have gone ashore there as forced the doors of Westerly. The doctor, although a kind man, could become very angry if roused, and he had made it plain that he would not tolerate trespassers.

It was impossible to land at the island except with a small boat like a skiff or dory, for the place was surrounded by shoals and rocks. On the side facing toward Westerly there lay a strip of sand, which was the only practical place to beach a boat, and here was planted a weathered sign, which said: TRESPASSERS WILL BE PROSECUTED.

For years this island, so close to the shore and sparsely wooded with pine trees and scrub oak, had been the doctor's private picnic spot, where he and his wife sometimes went to spend the day. Owlie remembered that as a little boy the place had fascinated him, and he had asked his father to take him over. But his father had said, "No, the doctor told me there was nothing that needed doing there, which meant I wasn't to go. Whether the doctor is here or whether he isn't, I carry out his wishes. I don't go myself, and I see that others don't." Owlie's father was like that.

Although Owlie for some years had been able to row a boat, he knew he was honor-bound to follow his father's example. Many times when the big house had been empty, he had taken a skiff round the island on a calm day, but he had never landed. From the water there had been nothing to see— only rocks and pines and the no-trespassing sign. But the island was big enough so that one couldn't tell what lay within the sheltering growth of trees.

Steps that crunched on the clamshell drive made him turn to see the stooped and weather-beaten figure of his father, trowel in hand, coming toward him. "Hello," Mr. Jennings said. "School's over; how do you like that?"

"Fine," said Owlie. He didn't know whether his father understood why he stopped off so frequently on his way home from school, for his father never talked much, just looked in a kindly way out of his keen gray eyes.

"Your mother baked some ginger cookies today," he said.

Owlie's eyes brightened behind his glasses. He smiled. "I guess I'll leave my books and lunch box in your car, Dad. I cleaned out my desk."

"Give them to me; I'll put them in. I'm going back to the garage for some rope."

"Thanks. See you later," Owlie said as he handed over the load he carried.

With his limping step the boy set off down the drive, feeling in his pocket for four lumps of sugar. By going only slightly out of his way, he could pass the fenced enclosure where Mr. Hammond kept saddle horses that he hired out to vacationers. Owlie liked to give the horses a treat, because they always looked tired and thin.

As he walked along the sunbaked road he whistled a tune and looked about him. Cottages were being opened up, and light trucks belonging to workmen stood in the driveways, some with ladders on top, some full of paint cans and tools.

Before the first of July he would start delivering the New York City papers to summer people, who any day now would begin arriving. The forty dollars that Owlie had earned last year was in the bank, and he planned to turn in his old bike and buy a new one that would be lighter and easier to pedal up the hills.

9

He turned down the lane toward home, his legs braced against the sharp descent.

As he walked along, scuffing the dust with his limping step, he noticed ahead of him a curious stone, gray with pink speckles, that looked as though it would make a good paperweight. When he reached it, he picked it up, spat on it, and rubbed the dust off on his trousers.

The stone had a nice feel to it. He shifted it from hand to hand, and his fingers moved over and around the smooth edges as he continued on his way. Suddenly he sniffed. The fresh sea air carried more and more strongly the pungent smell of horses —a mixture of straw and sweat and manure all blending into an exciting incense. He shifted the stone to his left hand while with his right hand he felt again for the sugar in his pocket.

Presently he turned off the lane and followed a short track which took him past a red barn in need of paint. Beyond that was an enclosure of white rails about four and a half feet in height, within which some horses were standing quietly in a far corner. They had the collapsed and dispirited air of livery stable animals that are used by bad riders who jerk their mouths and race them on hard ground. He liked to think that he could bring a little pleasure into their lives with his lumps of sugar. More than anything in the world he would have loved to ride one. Once he had asked Mr. Hammond how much it would cost, and the man had told him gruffly that it would be three dollars.

So Owlie contented himself with imagining that the horses were his. Each time he went there he would decide which one he would ride that day. Sometimes he chose to imagine himself on the black-and-white-spotted one, another day it would be the chestnut with the four white socks and the long thin neck, and then again he would have to decide between the black or the brown mare.

Today as the horses pricked their ears at the sight of him he noticed that a fifth horse had been added to the group of four. It was a bay with a black mane and tail who did not join the others as they strolled to the fence for their expected treat. Owlie thought this fortunate because he had only the four lumps of sugar. But he looked with interest at the bay, feeling he had added another horse to his string.

The animal's coat was dirty beyond words; its tail was full of burrs and its ribs showed through the rough coat. The bay needed cleaning so badly that it was hard to tell what sort of a horse it really was. Owlie was studying it, shifting the stone from one hand to the other when a sudden harsh voice made him jump. He looked up to find Bud standing beside him.

"Want to see some fun?" he asked. "Old Hammond's away; his truck's gone. Watch." He grinned, showing his broken tooth, and picking up a heavy piece of wood that lay nearby on the ground, he threw it into the midst of the quiet horses, who were still moving their lips to savor the sugar Owlie had given them.

"Stop!" cried Owlie, grabbing impulsively at Bud's arm. But the startled horses had set off at a laborious canter around the enclosure, and the bay, who had been standing alone, joined them.

Full of helpless fury he watched the frightened animals that had come to the fence so trustingly. The bay, now leading them, was galloping all out. In spite of his weak appearance he moved with a smoothness quite unlike the others that pounded clumsily behind him. As the galloping bay horse passed near the fence Bud stooped quickly, and picking up a big stone, hurled it at him with all his strength. The missile struck with a stinging thud full on the animal's flank, and to his horror Owlie saw the horse increase his speed as he neared the far boundary. He'll crash into the fence and hurt himself, he thought, tense with rage at Bud and in sympathetic agony for the horse. But to his amazement, with a clean leap the animal soared over the high rails and landed on the other side.

Owlie stood, his mouth open with astonishment. Suddenly he heard Bud give a muttered exclamation, then hiss below his breath, "Don't say it was me or I'll break every bone in your body next time I get you alone." And he was gone like a shadow around the corner of the barn just as Mr. Dover, Bud's father, appeared, walking rapidly from the opposite direction.

"Hey, what's going on here?" shouted Mr. Dover, his face very red. He advanced toward Owlie, swinging his huge shoulders as his eyes spotted the stone in the boy's hand.

"Throwing stones at horses! You deserve a good thrashing. Now get on home!" he commanded as he walked toward the bay, who was quietly cropping grass on the far side of the fence.

Mr. Dover approached the horse awkwardly, laid a hand on its halter, and opening a gate, led it back into the enclosure with the others.

"Look at that," he roared at Owlie, who had remained standing in the same spot by the fence.

"He's starting to go lame. Landed on a rock I shouldn't wonder. I won't tell Mr. Hammond on you this time because you're in the same class with Bud. But"—Mr. Dover's eyes narrowed and his dark eyebrows met over his thick nose—"if I ever catch you again at such tricks, I'll tell your father. Now beat it!"

Owlie was trembling as he turned away, his hand still automatically clutching the stone. He wanted to shout, I didn't do it, it was Bud. But Mr. Dover wouldn't have believed him, and he knew his tormentor would make it hard for him if he told the truth.

Futile rage and a deep sense of injustice choked in his throat as he set off toward home.

TWO

Hurrying down the steep lane, eager to get away from the sight and sound of Mr. Dover, Owlie saw ahead of him the low gray house, where he lived. Salt air had turned the shingles gray, while up the sides and over the roof rose vines made a cascade of red flowers, bright against the background of blue harbor water.

A white picket fence surrounded the house, and before the open gate stood a huge black dog.

"Hi, Sam," called Owlie.

At a clumsy canter the Newfoundland bounded up the slope, his enormous paws scattering the stones. When he reached Owlie, he bumped his broad head into the boy's stomach in a gesture of affection.

"Let's have a swim, eh, Sam?" Owlie patted the massive head pressed against him. Linking his fingers in the dog's collar, he walked the rest of the way home with the great beast padding beside him. Together they jostled through the gate, up the path, and on into the house, where the spicy smell of recent baking pleasantly greeted Owlie's nose. He laid his stone on the hall table.

Most boys would have called out, "Hi, Mom," but Owlie went straight toward the kitchen to find his mother, who would not have heard him if he had shouted. For, unfortunately, his mother had been stone deaf since birth.

He saw her standing by a table near the window near which a birdcage swung back and forth to the hops of a canary. She was putting ginger cookies into a deep crock.

Owlie came round in front of her so that she would not be startled and smiled into her eyes, which showed her happiness at the sight of him.

With one hand she made a quick gesture meaning, "Hello, son." Then she pointed toward the cookies and smiled. While she undid the bow of the clean checkered apron tied around her slim waist, she continued looking at him.

"Later," he spelled out to her with quick fingers and pointed to Sam.

His mother nodded, realizing he meant to have a swim first. She did not read lips easily, and her family had learned to communicate by forming letters with rapid motions of their fingers.

Owlie knew that even if his mother had been able to speak, she would not have used his nickname. When he was about four years old he had acquired the name by which everyone but his parents called him. It was on the day that he had walked back from the village optometrist, wearing his first pair of glasses.

A woman standing outside the grocery store, pinching the rosy cheeks of peaches in a basket, had said laughingly, "Why he looks like a dear little owl." Several people had overheard her, and the name had stuck.

By now Owlie had almost forgotten how the name had started. He just accepted the fact that practically no one in the world ever called him William.

Sam waited at the bottom of the stairs while Owlie ran up to change into his swimming trunks. The dog's enormous jaws gaped wide as he panted in anticipation of a swim. His tongue lolled out over sharp white teeth and saliva dripped from his wet lips. Although Sam looked like a ferocious black bear, he had the soul of a gentle sheep and he loved Owlie more than anyone in the world.

When the boy appeared at the top of the stairs, Sam's long tail, feathered with black fur, banged back and forth, hitting the bannister rail. Then he turned his great bulk around, almost upsetting a chair, and leaped joyously as the boy's bare feet thudded from the last step onto the rag rug of the hall.

In spite of being somewhat undersized, Owlie was wiry and strong. He stood straight in his blue swimming trunks, shoulders back, and it was only when he walked that his slight limp gave him the appearance of being handicapped.

The dog and the boy ran down the path together, through the gate, then over a short stretch of rough beach grass. When the bare brown feet and the thudding black paws reached the sand, they didn't stop but plunged on into the water, which deepened quickly.

Together the boy and the dog struck out, Owlie doing the crawl in a churning froth of water, the big dog beside him keeping abreast with underwater thrusts of his immense paws. Only his broad black head showed, lifted well up and cleaving a wake that rippled out behind him.

After a few moments Owlie flipped over on his back, stretched out his arms, and kicked his feet

19

gently in a slow float. His eyes had become accustomed to being without his glasses, and he felt he could see immense distances up into the snow-pudding clouds in the blue sky. It was only when Sam brought his head alongside that Owlie, turning to look at him, found that, as always, things close by were blurry.

With the great protective mass of Sam paddling near and the salt water buoying him up, all the resentment against Bud that had churned inside him floated away. He began to think with amazement of the tremendous leap the scrawny bay horse had taken and decided that next time he must bring along five lumps of sugar, for now he had an extra horse to feed. But he vowed he would never linger again beside the paddock rail unless he made certain that Mr. Hammond's truck was on the premises. Perhaps tomorrow he would stop by and find out if the bay horse was still lame.

A hollow feeling in his stomach made him imagine that he again smelled the freshly baked ginger cookies that waited for him in the kitchen; and he struck out for shore, racing Sam to the shallows, where he stood up and splashed to the beach beside the dripping dog.

Sam shook himself in the sunshine and a cloud of water sprayed into the air.

"If I were dry, I'd sure be soaking now, Sam. Thanks for the shower bath," said Owlie, slapping at the dog's wet flank. "Old Sambo-Bambo, you're as big as a pony. Remember how I used to ride on your back? I still could, I guess, but you might think I was a little heavy." Raising his arms, he flexed the muscles.

The dog lifted his head with a quick look, as if he'd understood.

Warm sand slid under Owlie's feet and powdered Sam's wet paws as they ran toward the house.

Now they were near enough for Owlie to notice the perfume of the roses that rioted all over the walls and roof, spilling bright blossoms among glossy green leaves.

As he opened the door he thought he could detect again that fresh-from-the-oven smell that meant ginger cookies. Leaning down before going in, he brushed the sand from his feet. "Stay there, Sam!" he commanded. "You're too wet."

The stone was still on the hall table. He had meant to give it to his mother for a paperweight, but somehow it had taken on the evil of that encounter with Bud and Mr. Dover. Not knowing quite what to do with it, he picked it up. A few drops of water fell onto the painted floor from his wet trunks, which had begun to drip dry on his run

21

from the beach. He smeared out the drops with his toe, then carrying the stone, he ran upstairs to change.

Owlie slept in a small room with a low ceiling that slanted lower still over the corner where his bed stood against a wall. Everything was so bright and cheerful that he always felt happy when he opened the door. A rag rug of many colors lay on the red-painted floor, pictures of horses and dogs and boats that he had cut from magazines were thumbtacked to the walls, and a big open bookshelf held not only books but a collection he had made, over the years, of abandoned birds' nests, interesting shells, and pieces of driftwood, worn by the sea to the shapes of serpents or animals. He put his stone on the edge of one of the shelves, then pushed it back out of sight behind a bird's nest.

It didn't take him long to dress in shorts, sneakers, and a sweat shirt. He found his large metal-rimmed glasses on top of the bureau, and as he put them on, everything in the room that had been blurry became clear and sharp.

Picking up a pencil and a thin book from a table beside his bed, he went to the casement of the door and stood very straight against it. He laid the book on top of his head, and fumbling with his right hand, made a mark behind him along the top edge of the book with the pencil. Then he removed the book from its precarious position on his head and examined the mark he had made. It was lower than a previous mark penciled above it. He was shrinking! Owlie felt a cold chill at his heart and quickly went back to his measuring position with the book on top of his head. He stretched every muscle upward until his neck muscles ached and was careful to draw the line straight above the book. He looked again. The new line had now darkened the old line. His disappointment at not having grown was swallowed up in the relief at not having shrunk, and he ran down to the kitchen with a light heart.

On the table his mother had set out a tall glass of milk beside a plate of ginger cookies. The soft warmness of the cookies and the cold tang of the milk mingled in his mouth and filled him with satisfaction.

He heard Sam's rumbling bark like a wind roaring out of a deep cave and knew the mailman must be at the door with the afternoon mail.

His mother came into the kitchen, carrying the letters and sorting them as she walked. There was a science magazine for Owlie which she handed to him, and then she held up a letter addressed to his father. The handwriting was Dr. Delafield's, and his mother smiled and nodded.

It was almost as if there were telepathic communication between the boy and his mother, for he knew at once what the smile meant and what she was thinking. "Isn't it splendid that the doctor feels strong enough to write?"

Owlie nodded emphatically, then spelled with quick flutters of his fingers, "Going out to the shed to clean my bike."

His mother gave an understanding nod, then turned to fill the water dish in the canary's cage.

Sam was waiting at the front door and greeted Owlie with one low bark and an enthusiastic tail wag. Together they walked toward a large dark green shed standing next to the garage in which Owlie's father kept their old station wagon.

The shed had two doors that swung outward. At one time the place might have been used for boat storage. There was a block and tackle hanging on one wall, and various tools such as rakes and spades were suspended from nails. It also housed the lawn mower and Owlie's bike, but mostly it was just waste space. A faint smell of tarred rope permeated the shadowy interior, which was lighted, when the doors were closed, by two small windows high in the walls at either end.

Owlie opened one of the doors, and he and the dog went inside. A battered old bicycle leaned against a wall, and the boy wheeled it out into the sunshine with the intention of oiling and cleaning it, so he could get more on a trade-in. Now that school was over he planned, probably the next day, to go up to the hardware store to see what kind of deal he could make.

He was working on the chain, using a piece of rag soaked in oil, when he looked up to see his father drive into the garage.

"Hi, Dad," called Owlie. "There's a letter from Dr. Delafield."

"Good!" exclaimed his father. "I'll let you know what he says."

Owlie went on working, using metal polish on the handlebars. Very shortly his father returned from the house carrying the letter. "Just like him," he said, waving the envelope back and forth. "He's giving the island for the summer to someone who needs a rest and fresh air. I'm to take over supplies."

"The island! That's funny," said Owlie, stopping his polishing to look at his father. "He's never allowed anyone on the island before."

"I know it. I don't understand it either. He says this person will run up a red flag when he wants something. I'm to find a list in a box on the shore by the no-trespassing sign. Aside from delivering what he wants, I'm not to bother him."

"He's probably a loony," said Owlie. "Maybe he's dangerous. How will he get to the island? That's what I'd like to know."

"The whole thing sounds queer," said his father, shaking his head doubtfully. "Still," he continued, "I've always followed out the doctor's wishes and no questions asked about things that are none of my business. These are his orders. All I have to do is watch for the flag to find out that the man has arrived."

"Maybe it's a woman," surmised Owlie.

"No, he said it was a man and he underlined the words *he wants to be left completely alone.*" His father examined the letter again, and again shook his head doubtfully. "He says to mail all bills for supplies to him, care of his bank in Chicago, and he will pay the man's expenses."

"Wow—pretty generous!" commented Owlie.

"Just like him if you ask me, son. Look at the people he used to ask down to visit him. Not his friends always. Some of them were pretty funny types who needed a vacation."

Owlie thought to himself, Lame ducks, but he

didn't say it aloud. There was something about those words that made them hard to say.

His father's lips were pressed together thoughtfully. "The island. No, I don't understand it," he said. "No one has ever been asked over there before."

"Yes, it's a funny thing," agreed Owlie.

"Well," said his father, stuffing the letter into his pocket, "we'll just have to keep a sharp lookout for the red flag."

THREE

Owlie was awakened by the wail of the fog horn on the point. He got out of bed and pressed his nose against the screen of his window, which was beaded with moisture. A thick fog had rolled in off the sea, and a hush lay over everything so that the least sound carried. He heard the clank of oars being dropped into a boat and figured his father had brought the big fisherman's dory alongside the dock. Probably he was going to row out and look at his lobster pots.

No matter what the weather, Owlie had decided to take his bike up to the village that morning and show it to the proprietor of the hardware store. There was an English bicycle he had seen through the window, but as yet he hadn't priced it. He hoped that with his forty dollars plus the trade-in of his old bike he could afford the new one he admired.

"You'd better put on your oilskins. It's as wet as if it were raining," his mother spelled out with her fingers as he finished his breakfast and started toward the door.

"I'll be all right, Mom," Owlie spelled back. "Keep Sam in, will you? I'm going up to the village. He howls if I don't take him inside the store."

It was really harder to pedal his bike up the lane than to push it, but Owlie had a self-imposed program that he felt would promote growth and strength, and bicycle pedaling was part of it.

The thick mist lay over everything and drifted in ghostly swirls. He felt isolated in a pocket of dampness. Bud Dover's house was almost invisible from the lane as he passed it, and he hoped that on his first day of vacation Bud was still asleep.

In his eagerness to price the new bike he had forgotten momentarily how early it was, but suddenly he realized that the shop wouldn't be open yet. In that case it would be fun to visit the horses. The track that ran off toward the stable lay just ahead. If only he had thought, he would have brought some sugar! It seemed to him mean to disappoint the poor animals by appearing at the fence with nothing to offer them.

On a bank farther up the lane he remembered seeing a heavy growth of clover where someone must have dumped a load of good soil or dropped a bag of fertilizer. Anyway, clover grew lush and green at this one spot, quite unlike the grass and weeds that struggled for existence in the sandy soil along the rest of the lane. When he came to the place, Owlie broke off juicy stalks, wet with fog, as carefully as if he were gathering a bunch of flowers. Soon he had a good handful.

He left his bike where he had dropped it and walked back toward the red barn.

Mr. Hammond, whose wizened neck emerged from a soiled turtleneck sweater, was standing in the middle of the enclosure, looking with disgust at the bay horse. He bent to feel his near foreleg as Owlie came up to the fence. Seeing the boy, he greeted him sourly with a curt "Good morning."

The other horses had noticed the fistful of clover stalks Owlie held in his hand and started toward the fence, led by the black mare. With quiet motions Owlie distributed two or three stalks to each as they shoved at each other for place. The chestnut, with ears laid back, tried to get more than his share and Owlie pushed him off. "Hey, no, you can't have all of it," he said, stepping back and preserving a few stems and leaves, for he had noticed the bay coming toward him with a painful limp that made the horse's head nod as he walked.

Perhaps there was something about that limp that reminded him of his own, or perhaps it was a look in the horse's eyes, half fearful of what Owlie would do to him, that made the boy's heart go out to the lame animal as it approached. He stroked the horse's nose and gently pulled at his unkempt forelock while the hungry creature munched on the rich green clover. Beads of moisture from the heavy mist clung to the fine hair of the horse's ears, which were cool to Owlie's touch.

Mr. Hammond, apparently feeling the need of talking to someone, walked across the enclosure to Owlie's side. "Dag drat it," he said crossly. "What a piece of bad luck! Here I bought this danged horse just yesterday and now goodness knows why, but he's gone lame. He'll never be ready for hard work this summer, and I can't keep him around eating his head off when he's not earning anything."

Hmm, thought the boy bitterly, "eating his head off" is good. I'll bet Mr. Hammond's horses don't get much more than some old moldy hay. But he kept quiet and listened to the man's complaints.

"I bought this animal yesterday from a farmer.

Said he was sick and tired of his jumping out of the pasture. Neighbors had complained about him getting into their vegetable gardens and eating the peas. He was shut up in the barn when I saw him. I only paid forty dollars for him, but now he's not worth that." Mr. Hammond struck at the horse in disgust, and the animal flung up his head and backed away.

"Bowed tendon he's got," continued Mr. Hammond furiously. "No good whatever to me. Summer people going to come any day now. What use is a horse you can't rent out? I'm not going to pay any veterinary bills. I'm going in to call the mink farm to come and get him for meat." Mr. Hammond turned away with an angry grunt and started toward the barn.

Forty dollars. There was something about the sound of the very sum he had in the bank that electrified Owlie. He opened his mouth, but no sound came out. What could he possibly do with a horse?

The bay horse moved his head and looked toward Mr. Hammond's retreating figure then turned and took a step toward Owlie. He had such beautiful wide-set brown eyes, a broad brow denoting intelligence, neat short ears. Owlie's glance raced

32

over the bony frame and found it beautiful. Something stronger than reason took possession of him. This horse must not die. He climbed the fence in pursuit of Mr. Hammond.

"Hey, Mr. Hammond," he called, "if I give you forty dollars, can I have him?"

The man stopped dead in his tracks and looked at the boy. "Are you crazy?" he asked.

"I'll have the money here in a half an hour, just as soon as the bank opens. I have my bank book." From his pocket he pulled the slim folder and offered it as evidence.

Mr. Hammond looked at him. "Well, they say there's a fool born every minute," he remarked. "I guess I'm looking at one that was born around a dozen years ago."

"Don't call the meat man, will you," urged Owlie. "I'll be back in a second."

"Oh, I won't call him, don't you worry," drawled Mr. Hammond, "but don't say I didn't warn you. If this is a bowed tendon, and it sure looks like it, this horse will have to be fired. Anyhow, I wish I'd never gotten him. He looks like the kind if you fed him up he'd be hard to ride. No good in my line of business."

For one lucid moment Owlie realized the madness of what he was doing. He who had never even been on the back of a horse in his life was about to invest every cent he owned in one.

Too late now to change his mind. He hurried away to the lane and picked up his bike from the bed of clover. Pumping along toward the village, he heard a bell buoy tolling somberly somewhere out at sea as it heaved on slow swells, warning fogbound boats.

He passed the hardware store and saw, gleaming with beautiful newness, the English bicycle he had hoped to purchase that morning. It was hard not to stop.

Choking back his misgivings, he entered the bank and drew out four crisp ten-dollar bills, which he folded and slid into the pocket of his blue jeans.

Mr. Hammond was waiting. He apparently had believed Owlie, for he had put an old bridle on the horse and was standing with him by the fence.

The boy pulled the money out of his pocket and thrust it at the man.

"What are you going to do with your bike?" asked Mr. Hammond.

"I'll pick it up later," said Owlie, who up to then hadn't figured that far ahead. Something had been troubling him deeply on his ride from the bank. "What's firing?" he asked.

"Oh, you get a vet to stick hot needles into the

swelling on the leg, and that usually clears it up. Pretty often the critter isn't much good afterward," said Mr. Hammond gloomily.

The boy gazed uncertainly at the horse he had just bought.

"Want a leg up?" asked Mr. Hammond.

"Sure," said Owlie with a voice that was only a whisper.

Suddenly he found himself sitting on the horse's back, although he wasn't quite certain how he'd gotten there.

"Well, so long," said Mr. Hammond, opening the gate.

Owlie was speechless, but he guided his horse, who seemed more than willing to leave Mr. Hammond's company, out the gate and past the red barn. He felt the man eyeing him, so he sat very straight, squeezing the horse's bony ribs with his legs, ready to reach any moment for the mane to steady himself.

Near panic struck him as he turned into the lane. Where was he going to put his horse? What would his mother and father say?

Sam had plenty to say as he saw the limping horse approaching. His deep-throated bark warned of something extraordinary going on.

Owlie called out. "Hi, Sam. Come here, Sam."

When the big dog approached at a slow and cautious walk, the horse pricked up his ears but didn't act alarmed. Sam came alongside and sniffed warily at the horse's legs, but still the horse registered no objection. "Maybe he thinks Sam's a pony," Owlie speculated.

After a moment the Newfoundland wagged his tail and looked up. Not bad, he seemed to say.

A little of the weight lifted from the boy's heart as Sam accepted the new member of the family. But just at that moment the door of the house opened and his mother came outside.

At the vision of her son on a horse she stood transfixed with amazement. Then, apparently finding it a wonderful sight, she clapped her hands together in pleasure and made a sign. "Who?"

There was no mistaking what she meant. Whose horse are you riding? she wanted to know.

It being beyond him at the moment to signal back "Mine," he pretended he hadn't understood and waved his hand gaily.

As if remembering something that might boil over on the stove, his mother turned quickly back into the house, and at that moment his father came round the corner from the dock, carrying the oars from the dory over his shoulder. It had always been his practice never to appear surprised. He laid the oars down slowly and carefully by the picket fence, then turning with an unhurried step, he approached Owlie and the horse.

"Who lent you that?" he asked quietly, all the time running an eye over the animal's gaunt frame.

Owlie turned pale. He swallowed the words that stuck in his throat and said nothing.

With a firm and quiet hand his father felt down all the horse's four legs. "Looks like he's sprained the tendon on his near fore," he remarked.

"Mr. Hammond says it's bowed," said Owlie, finding his voice.

"Nothing so serious as that I'd say. Old Hammond owns horses, but he doesn't know much about them. How did he happen to let you bring the horse down here? He needs cold water on that leg; he shouldn't be ridden."

"He was going to sell him to the mink farm for meat!" Owlie's voice shook with indignation. "So I—well, I—well, I just bought him."

The man's keen gray eyes in his weathered face took one look at his son.

"Might be a nice horse if he had some flesh on him," he said softly.

Owlie's heart, which had sunk as far down as

a heart can sink without disappearing altogether, gave a leap upward. He gave his father a smile full of love and gratitude.

"Dad, I didn't know you knew anything about horses."

"When I was around your age, son, I worked summers for a man who had a stable. I got to know a little about them. Where do you plan to keep this animal?"

"I—I hadn't thought," said Owlie, again looking worried and uncertain.

"Son," said his father, "it's all right to have good impulses, but it's better to think before you act."

"Yes, I know," said Owlie weakly.

"Perhaps we could build a stall for him in the shed," mused his father. "How were you planning to feed him? I imagine you spent all your savings to buy him."

"Well, yes," said Owlie. "I thought I could get him food with the money I'll get from my paper route this year."

"No harm in letting him eat grass around the place, though it's not very good on this sandy soil. What he needs are some oats and good hay. He's looking awfully poor at the moment. Too bad we don't have a fenced-in field."

"It wouldn't do any good," said Owlie, "he

39

jumps out of everything. That's why the man sold him to Mr. Hammond."

"Wouldn't be surprised if somebody had been shutting him up in a barn with no feed at all," said his father. He looked straight at his son. "Let's see what we can do to bring him back," he said.

"Oh, yeah, Dad, that will be great!" cried Owlie fervently. The load of guilt and anxiety that had oppressed him suddenly vanished when he knew himself to be in partnership with his father.

A thoughtful look came over his parent's face and Owlie, knowing him, kept quiet, for he understood his father's ways. Never did he rush into a job without first thinking the situation through. Then when at last he had decided on a plan, he would proceed with sure motions to carry it out.

All at once the horse, tired of standing, moved a few steps forward, jerked his head down to the grass and pulled the reins out of Owlie's hand. Its lowered neck looked like a long toboggan slide to the ground and the boy grabbed a piece of mane with one hand and with the other retrieved the sliding reins. But he did not attempt to pull up the horse's head, for with ravenous jerks the animal was snatching at the sparse grass outside the fence.

"Well, son"—his father's voice sounded full of decision—"this is how I figure it. We can tie this horse up in the shed when the time comes, but first it strikes me there are two things we need to accomplish. The first is to get him some food, and the second is to tend to that leg. I wouldn't try to buy any hay or grain from Hammond—his hay would be moldy I'll bet, and his grain would be mostly husks. No, there's a lucky thing I happen to remember. Last time I went over to Beachport I saw a new sign at the lumber company saying they were selling hay and grain. Now how do you figure you'd pay if I should say I was willing to go over there this afternoon with the station wagon and pick up a load?"

Owlie's face became troubled. He screwed up his eyes and pursed his lips. Finally he looked at his father. "I don't know," he said frankly.

"I don't imagine Tod Doan at the lumber company is giving away hay and grain for nothing," said his father. "Have you a plan to suggest?"

"Could you lend me the money, Dad?" Owlie's voice was anxious. He looked down the side of the horse's lowered neck, saw the eager mouth snatching for the poor grass, and realized how hungry the animal must be. He imagined him burying his nose in a quart of yellow oats. "Or I could sell my bike," he suggested.

"How would you deliver your papers?"

"On my horse," said Owlie stoutly, and at the very thought he turned pale. It had taken all his nerve to ride the horse home down the familiar lane.

"Well now, son, I'll tell you how this situation appears to me. If you had gone out and bought this horse for yourself just because you wanted him, I would say that you had done a very rash and thoughtless thing. But as it is, I must say I have a lot of sympathy for what you did. This is a good horse; it would have been terrible to make him into meat for a mink farm without giving him a chance."

Owlie's face brightened. "As soon as I start my paper route, I'll pay you back if you'll advance me the money," he promised.

"If you borrow money from a bank they charge you about six per cent," said his father.

"I'll pay you interest," said Owlie.

His father looked approvingly at him, then he smiled. "Let's say that it being all in the family, we'll skip the interest."

"What about his leg?" asked Owlie. "I guess I'd better keep my bike because he's too lame to ride on a paper route."

His father looked at the horse. "He should have cold water on it to take down that swelling."

"You don't think he'll have to be fired?" asked Owlie anxiously.

His father once more ran a hand down the lame leg. "No, I don't," he said positively. "In my opinion it's no more than a bad sprain. If we could get him to stand in the water with you on his back, it would be a wonderful thing. Shall we try it?"

Owlie swallowed hard. "Sure," he said huskily.

"Lucky I have on my rubber boots," said his father, reaching down and taking hold of the horse's bridle. "Come on," he said quietly, pulling the eager head away from the grass. "Pretty soon we'll have something for you that will taste better than that."

The horse, seeming to sense the man's kindness and authority, followed quietly as he was led toward the beach with Owlie still aboard. But when they reached the sand, he stopped and looked with surprise at the succession of ripples that ran toward him and then retreated.

The boy patted his neck encouragingly while his father urged the horse forward. Hesitating, the

animal blew through his nose with fear and moved sideways a few steps so that Owlie was almost dislodged. Then suddenly, with no further resistance, he consented to follow the man into the water, lowering his head and pricking his ears as if listening to the plops his feet made. They stopped a few yards off shore.

"Try to keep him right there until I get back. It will take me about half an hour round trip to Beachport." His father let go of the bridle.

Owlie nodded. He thought of the English bicycle still sitting in that window. He thought of how he had intended to go whizzing along the road on fast-turning wheels. Instead he had bought something as lame as himself. For a moment he felt rather sick, but loyally he smoothed the horse's black mane and began to pick out some of the burrs.

"If he hasn't a name yet, you'd better give him one," called his father as he waded ashore.

Sam had lain down in the shallows. His gaze was fixed on Owlie, and his tail splashed the water from time to time.

The horse stood quietly. Perhaps the cool salt water felt good on his swollen leg. The boy looked out over the glassy surface of the harbor. Midmorning sun was burning off the fog and the round disk, high on the horizon, looked like the glow from a heater in a steamy shower room. It was a quiet day—no wind and the water dead still. He stared up harbor toward Dr. Delafield's island, then pulled off his glasses, for he always felt he could see farther without them. His eyes searched for a red flag against the green of the pines. But there was nothing—only two white gulls that circled above the gray rocks and mewed with catlike cries.

FOUR

The shed was now called "the stable" and a great transformation had taken place there. The whole interior had been whitewashed, giving it a light, clean appearance; and the two windows, which were high enough so that there was no direct draft, were opened to allow for ventilation when the doors were shut. In one corner an enclosure of boards with a swinging door made a box stall, and the smell of tarred rope, which had always permeated the shed, was almost drowned out by the sweet smell of the hay that stood ranged in bales along one wall. A deep bed of golden straw covered the earthen floor of the stall, and a pile of hay had been forked into a corner.

"The Ritz," said Owlie's father. "Positively a horse hotel." His gray eyes were full of half-amused satisfaction as he stood looking through the open doors. Father and son had worked every evening after supper with saw and hammer and nails to achieve this neat workmanlike stable, and afternoons Owlie had whitewashed the walls when he wasn't sitting on his horse out in the healing salt water.

He had begun his paper route, so mornings were pretty well taken up with delivering the New York papers to fifteen different houses. And he had hopes of more customers in August. With the money he earned, he was gradually paying back the loan that had been made him for feed.

"What are you going to call that horse?" asked his father.

"I haven't decided yet," said Owlie.

"You're taking a long time, son. We can't call him *the horse* forever, can we?"

"No. I've been thinking. What about King Edward?"

"Why King Edward? It's your horse and you name him what you want to, but why do you like that name?"

"We studied about Edward the Third of England. He was awfully brave. He was always fighting battles. You know, the battle of Crécy and everything. Besides, I like the name Edward."

His father scowled thoughtfully. "An ancestor of yours fought in the American Revolution to get rid of kings."

"Oh," said Owlie. "You think *Mr.* Edward would be more free and equal, more American?" He smiled.

"Too long," said his father. "And somehow Edward doesn't sound exactly like a horse's name. Mr. E. is more the right length but I don't like it much, do you?"

"Mr. E." mused Owlie. "Mr. E—Mystery-y. Mystery!" he almost shouted. "Hey, that's good! You said it was a mystery where such a good horse came from."

"Not bad," agreed his father. "I like the name. Mystery it is?"

"Yes," said Owlie.

The two of them stood watching the horse whose head, ears pricked up, was turned toward them over the top of the stall.

"I think you like your name, don't you, Mystery?" said Owlie's father. Suddenly he faced about and moved toward his car. "Can't stand here and admire your horse all day. I've got to get my work done. I'll see you later, son. I'm running over to Beachport to pick up some nails. They don't have the kind I want in the village. I'll be back about two o'clock."

"Do you think it would be all right if I rode Mystery down the beach aways this afternoon?"

"Go ahead. You might ride him into the water every once in awhile to keep that leg cool. I wouldn't go faster than a walk yet though."

"No, I won't."

"Good-bye."

"Good-bye." Owlie watched his father drive away, then turned toward Mystery, who was tethered between two willow trees in front of the stable. They had rigged up a rope along which ran a ring, and his halter rope was tied to this, enabling him to walk up and down. It was long enough so he could nibble at a little hay they tossed on the ground but short enough to prevent him from getting his leg caught. All the time Owlie and his father were working to transform the shed into a stable, the horse had watched them through the open doors as they worked inside and had seemed to enjoy their company. Owlie would come out every once in awhile to pat him, talk to him, or feed him a carrot, an apple, or a lump of sugar.

"Too much sugar is bad," his father had cautioned.

Owlie thought how his mother was always after him about candy and soft drinks. "Have a piece of fruit or a glass of milk instead," she would urge him in her sign language. Apparently horses were the same as boys. Fresh natural food was best.

He pulled some grass a little distance from where his horse was tied, then offered it on the palm of his hand. The soft nibbling lips felt nice and tickly as Mystery gathered up the scattered blades.

"Let's you and Sam and me go for a walk," he suggested.

The dog, who was lying nearby, moved his ears, wagged his tail alertly, then heaved his great bulk up onto his massive paws and watched Owlie go to the stable to bring back the old bridle, which had undergone cleaning and polishing. With deft motions the boy laid the reins over the horse's neck, then slipped off the rope halter he and his father had made and replaced it with the bridle.

Now it was time to mount and Owlie was ready to perform a trick he had been practicing off and on for days. As he had no saddle and always rode bareback, an easy mounting with stirrups was out of the question, and the only practical answer was to vault onto the horse's back. Because of his lame left leg he stood with that foot on a slight rise, bringing his legs even.

While Sam watched and the horse stood patiently, Owlie gathered up the reins in his left hand, which he rested on the withers; then with

51

a spring up, he flung his right leg over the horse's back and tugging at the mane, he maneuvered himself into an upright position.

A look of triumph illumined his face as he gazed down from his lofty perch at big black Sam, whose tail beat back and forth and whose brown eyes looked with adoration at his clever master, who could fly through the air and land on a horse.

Mystery's backbone was rather prominent due to his poor condition, and Owlie, squeezing with his legs, raised himself up for a moment to gain some comfort. He had been in the habit of doing this while they stood out in the water, and the frequent rising and sitting had strengthened the boy's legs until his seat on the horse was far more secure than it had been on that day when he had teetered down the lane from Mr. Hammond's, clutching at the horse's mane for support.

Because a two-week's diet of oats had brightened Mystery's spirits perceptibly, Owlie sat alert and ready to check any desire to trot, remembering his father's caution.

They made their way slowly along the shore, keeping close to the water, with the horse's hoofs plopping on the wet sand and leaving crescent-shaped marks that were quickly erased by small waves coming ashore. The dog, following a little farther out, seemed to enjoy the feel of water on his paws and did not mind the sudden spray thrown into his face when Owlie, taking his father's advice to keep cooling the leg, guided Mystery into deeper water.

Gulls circled overhead in the sunshine, emitting their strident cries as they planed back and forth on air currents. A sandpiper ran down the beach, darting on thin legs after a receding wave and pecking with his long bill to find food among the shells and seaweed. There was a nice fishy, salty smell all around that Owlie liked.

Today his horse was walking sound, with long easy strides. No longer did the boy have to endure a repetition of his own limp. Instead the strong legs under him made him feel freer and more alive than ever before in his life.

Sun danced on the water and glinted silver on low waves coming gently ashore. Owlie's half-opened shirt fluttered against his chest in the light wind. He breathed in all the satisfaction he felt and filled his lungs with salt air.

Their walk along the sand was bringing them nearer Westerly, and ahead he could see the steep flight of wooden steps that dropped from the cliff to the beach.

Off to his left out in the harbor lay the island,

where the gray rocks and green pines appeared as quiet and isolated as usual, ringed with blue water.

But all at once he was brought up short by a sudden sight, and he instinctively pulled Mystery to a stop.

Slowly rising against the green of the island pines, a red pennant fluttered, jerked, rose, to the full height of a pole, then streamed out in the wind that was blowing stronger now from the sea.

Owlie whipped his glasses off his face and strained his eyes trying to discern the figure of a man. It seemed to him there was a movement of some sort among the trees, but he couldn't be sure. The only certain thing was the flag that was summoning his father, and he turned his horse to ride back and report.

Beside the stable he found the old station wagon parked near a car he had never seen before.

"Hey, Dad!" he called.

In answer to his shout he saw his father emerge from the stable followed by a man whose red and cheerful face broke into a smile at the sight of the dog, the horse, and the boy.

"The flag's on the island," said Owlie abruptly.

His father nodded slowly. Everything in good

time, he conveyed to his son by that slow nod. "This is Dr. Little, the vet," he said.

"How are you, fellow?" asked the big ruddy man. "Your father says he doesn't think your horse is picking up fast enough. He wants me to have a look at him."

Owlie slid to the ground and stood holding Mystery, his right hand up close to the bridle, his left hand holding the end of the reins he had pulled over the horse's head.

"I saw Dr. Little in Beachport," explained his father. "I told him we had a horse at our place. He said he would stop round and take a look at him."

The vet was running his big gentle hands along Mystery's flanks and down his legs. Then he grasped his upper and lower jaws, opened them, and peering into his mouth, examined his teeth and gums.

"About six years old," he said. "I'd say he has a bad case of worms. Lots of horses who have been turned out on poor pasture land have them."

"What do you do about that?" asked Owlie worriedly.

"Give him a pill," said the vet with a brisk decisive nod. He went to his car and came back with what looked to Owlie like a gun, which he began to load, not with a bullet but with a brownish-colored pill about the size of the end of his thumb.

"Well, young man," he said, "how would you like to be a vet for a minute. This is your horse. We don't need Dad to do the job, do we?" With seeming nonchalance he led the horse toward a bank so that Owlie could stand higher than the animal's head and handed him the loaded gun. "When I open his mouth, push the muzzle in on top of his tongue and fire," he directed.

With nervous fingers the boy took the proffered gun, determined to do as he had been told.

When the vet seized Mystery's jaws and pulled them open, the horse rolled his eyes and laid back his ears, but before he could pull away, Owlie had thrust the gun into his throat and squeezed the trigger.

"There," said the vet, letting go of the horse and patting his neck. "That will kill those worms, and he'll get the benefit of his food. His coat will have some life in it, and his eyes will brighten up." He laid a heavy hand on Owlie's shoulder. "You did all right, boy. Perhaps you'll be a vet some day."

Owlie beamed. He was experiencing a warm feeling of satisfaction at having performed adequately the task he had been assigned.

"It's too bad I don't know anything about riding," said Owlie's father. "I used to take care of horses when I was a youngster but I can't give my boy any pointers on how to ride one."

"He looked pretty comfortable sitting on the horse when I saw him," remarked the vet.

"His backbone's awfully sharp," said Owlie, making a face.

"Your father told me you didn't have a saddle, that you'd taught yourself to ride bareback. It just occurred to me that you could use this." Dr. Little had reached into the back of his car, and pulling with both hands, he extracted an English saddle with stirrups and girth attached. "I took this in payment from someone who was short of cash. It belonged to his son, who had stopped riding. I don't mind if you borrow it for a while."

"Wow!" said Owlie. "Thanks!"

"When this worm medicine takes hold and your horse is getting the benefit from his grain, he's going to have some life in him. I imagine you'll stay topside better at a trot and canter if you've got a saddle." Dr. Little was running his hand down the horse's near foreleg. "Almost well," he nodded. "Hammond's a fool. He's going to be furious that he sold this horse. He may try to get him back."

"He's mine," said Owlie. "I paid for him."

The vet nodded in a preoccupied way. He was standing off and regarding the horse with a critical eye, seeming to take in every detail of his conformation.

"Hmm," he said finally, scratching his head as if to stir up his brains. "I think I've seen this horse before. I'm beginning to think I know who he is."

The noise of a screen door slamming made them all look up to see Owlie's mother coming out of the house carrying a tray laden with glasses of lemonade and sandwiches. Her flowered-print dress was freshly washed and ironed, her brown hair neatly combed, and her whole face radiated the pleasure she felt in bringing something she knew would be enjoyed.

"My wife is a deaf mute," said Owlie's father hastily.

The vet gave a quick nod. Smiling cordially, he took the tray from the woman's hands.

"Looks good," he enunciated elaborately and he smiled, nodding his head with emphasis.

His cordiality was understood and appreciated. Owlie's mother nodded and motioned for everyone to find a seat on benches drawn up beside a table under one of the willow trees.

Mystery was put into his halter, and he watched the picnic with a rather annoyed expression in his eyes as he mouthed over a strange taste. Owlie guessed that fumes must be rising from his stomach due to the pill that was starting its good work.

Trailing willow branches swayed above their heads and flecks of sun that penetrated the shade glinted on the glasses of lemonade.

Dr. Little helped himself to a proffered egg-and-olive sandwich. "I'm sure now that I know that horse," he said, "and it's a strange story. Sometimes I get called pretty far away on a case, and I remember about three years ago I was asked to go to a farm around fifty miles from here where a mare was having difficulty foaling. The people didn't have much confidence in their local vet; said he was better with dogs than horses. So I went and everything turned out all right; a nice little filly was born."

Owlie's father, with quick motions of his fingers, was giving his wife the gist of what the vet was telling, and with smiles and nods she showed her interest.

Dr. Little leaned back comfortably against the tree trunk, took a sip of his lemonade, and continued. "I remember there was a girl of about ten, who was riding a nice-looking bay colt when I arrived. She was cantering around a field, and then I saw her stop under an apple tree and try to reach for some fruit. Well, she couldn't reach what she wanted, so I remember she dropped the reins on the colt's neck, stood up in the saddle, and picked a couple of apples. All the time, mind you, this colt was standing perfectly still. They just seemed to understand each other. When she dropped back into the saddle, she bit off a piece from one of the apples and reached down the horse's neck to give it to him. You could see he knew what to expect. He turned his head and took the piece as nice as you please.

"While I was tending to the mare I asked the father about the colt, and he told me he was out of the quarter horse mare who was foaling that day. She was a nice animal, very gentle. The sire was Bolt from the Blue, who had won a lot of steeplechases." The vet took a bite of his sandwich and then sipped his lemonade.

Sam had flopped down, and his great head rested on Owlie's foot. Every once in awhile he twitched an ear as if he were listening. The boy had laid a hand on the dog's head, but his eyes were on his horse, standing quietly under the willow tree and whisking away an occasional fly with his tail. His ribs still showed, but his eyes had lost the frightened look they had had when he belonged to Mr. Hammond.

"I was sorry," continued Dr. Little, "when I heard from a fellow one day that those nice people had had to move from the farm into the city. The father had a slipped disc in his back and couldn't do heavy work anymore. The bay colt, who was about four by then, had been sold to someone who promised to give him a good home. But he got passed along, as so often happens; owner decided to play golf or some such nonsense. Next thing I heard, a year later, he was being auctioned off, and I was interested enough to go around to bid on him. But I was delayed by an emergency call —a dog had been run over—and by the time I arrived, the horse had been sold to a farmer. Someone said he was going to use him to haul potatoes."

"That must have been the farmer Mr. Hammond bought him from!" exclaimed Owlie excitedly.

"Well, you see you've got a good horse, a really good horse. He's going to take some riding when he feels well," said Dr. Little, smiling. "And another thing you can be thankful for, young fellow, that horse was started right. He's met with abuse in the last year, but he started off with confidence, and that's a great thing for anybody, animal or person."

Owlie's father put a hand on his son's shoulder and his eyes had a kindly twinkle. "You did all right," he said. "I don't know how *useful* this animal's going to be, but it looks as if before long he's going to be ornamental."

Dr. Little rose to leave and bowed politely. Then he looked at Owlie's father. "You gave me good directions to get to your house, but do you know, I don't think I know your name. I should. I've seen you around Beachport more than once."

"Jennings, Thomas Jennings." Owlie's father shook the vet's hand. "How much do I owe you?"

"I hate to talk business after these nice refreshments," said the vet.

"No, no! Come on, what do I owe you? Look here, you've lent my boy a saddle. I can't have this—what do I owe you?"

"Five dollars then," said Dr. Little. His eyes were on Mystery. "You'll be surprised at what that horse will look like when he fattens up and his coat improves. Do you have a grooming kit?"

"No," said Owlie, "I brush him off with a whisk

broom and a rag. I picked the burrs out of his tail."

The vet smiled and accepted the five dollars Thomas Jennings pushed into his hand. "You'll never make him shine that way. You need a curry comb, a dandy brush, a body brush, a tail comb, and a hoof pick. After you get them, let me know, and I'll stop by someday to show you how to use them."

"Thank you, Dr. Little," said Owlie. "I think my father knows how to use them too." He wanted to say, Keeping a horse is expensive, that's why we don't have all those things, but instead he turned and patted his horse's flank, where the rough dull coat was indeed in need of a good grooming.

"Feed him regularly," directed the vet, "three feeds a day and about five buckets of water. Some people don't realize a horse needs more meals than a dog and that he requires a lot of water. His feet need attention too. I'll ask the blacksmith to stop by someday. Good-bye and good luck. I wish I knew more about riding myself so I could give you some pointers."

Thomas Jennings stood politely until the vet's car left the place. He gave one farewell motion of his hand as it turned up the lane. Then he faced his son and smiled slowly, as if he was proud of him. But all he said was, "It's about three-thirty. I'm going to row over to the island; I'll be back in half an hour."

"Do you think you'll find a list inside that old box the doctor said the man would use?"

"Well, it had better be there, or the fellow won't get anything to eat. Not unless he shoots sea gulls, and I should think they'd be pretty tough."

"Besides, it's against the law to shoot sea gulls," said Owlie.

"That's right; they're scavengers," agreed his father.

"Do you think you'll see the man?" asked Owlie.

"Shouldn't think so," said his father.

FIVE

"Here he comes, back from the island," spelled Owlie's mother as she took from her son's hand a basket full of fresh peas he had just picked in their vegetable garden.

Owlie went to meet the slightly stooped figure walking up from the dock with the oars over his shoulder. "Did you find anything, Dad?" he asked.

"There was a box right by the no-trespassing sign, just where the doctor said the man would put it. Here's the list I found." Owlie's father pushed a piece of paper into his son's hand. Printed carefully in block letters, the items were easy to read.

> KEROSENE
> BACON
> BREAD
> SOAP
> BUTTER
> DOZ. CANS OF MILK
> COFFEE

DOZ. CANS PORK AND BEANS
MOLASSES
CHEESE
JAM
6 CANS OF PEAS
PEANUT BUTTER
EGGS
DOZ. CANS VEGETABLE SOUP
A COOKED HAM

"Did you see him?" asked Owlie.

His father shook his head. "You wouldn't want to go to the village and get that kerosene for me, would you? I can pick up the rest of the things at the grocery on my way to Westerly."

"Sure," said Owlie. "May I row over with you when you take the stuff after supper?"

"That's a good idea. We'll use the dory. We'd never get all these supplies in the skiff. Here's five dollars. You'll have to buy a can for the kerosene. I could buy it myself, but it will save some time if you do it. Your mother likes us to be prompt for supper, as we both know." His father smiled. "Her suppers are worth being prompt for."

"Lamb and fresh peas tonight," said Owlie. "She's making a lemon pie too."

"I'll hurry," said his father, moving, however, at his usual deliberate pace toward the station wagon.

Owlie set off with his quick limping step. He didn't think it would be very practical to ride his bike and swing a big can from the handle bars. He took a short cut through an empty lot.

The path he followed took him past the ball field, and as he drew near he could hear shouts of "Run! Run!" Then groans, and "He's out!"

As he came within sight of the field he saw Bud Dover standing by the plate, spitting on his hands and rubbing them in the dust. Owlie watched him pick up the bat and swing it back and forth, getting the feel as he waited for Roy Bladen to warm up for the pitch.

A skinny boy, whose cap was on backward, was standing on the sidelines, punching a catcher's mitt. "Hi, Owlie," he said in a listless tone.

"Hi," said Owlie, and he trudged on, trying to disguise his limp as much as possible.

Just then the bat connected with a crack that sent up a shout, and Owlie looked back over his shoulder to see the ball in the air descending in his direction. Instinctively he turned and concentrated each fiber of his being on catching it. It was as if every rebuff he had suffered at the hands of his classmates tautened his nerves to show them what he could do.

He heard shouts in the distance but didn't realize what they meant. Keeping his eyes fixed desperately on the ball, he held out his hands till he felt the sting of rawhide, then closed his fingers convulsively and found that he held the ball.

A feeling of elation surged within him, but his triumph was cut short as he began to sort out what the boys were shouting at him.

"You dope, Owlie, you weren't in the game!" yelled Red Wilson.

"He caught a fly ball! You're out, Bud!" screamed the skinny boy.

"No, I'm not out! It's not fair. Owlie isn't in the game!" shouted Bud. "I might have made a home run if it wasn't for that dumbbell."

Owlie's cheeks burned with mortification as he stood undecided, holding the ball in his hand.

"Throw it here," yelled Roy.

Owlie took an awkward step and threw the ball jerkily so that it hit the ground a few yards from him. Roy had to walk forward to retrieve it.

"That was a good catch, Owlie," he said kindly. "Especially without a glove."

Bud Dover was grinning and making rapid motions with his fingers in imitation of the sign language of a deaf mute.

Owlie turned away quickly, pretending he hadn't seen. He pushed his glasses up on his nose and tramped off looking as unconcerned as possible and whistling tunelessly.

After purchasing a red can full of kerosene, he walked back the long way by the road and arrived only a few minutes ahead of his father.

Although he had looked forward to the good supper he knew his mother was preparing, somehow when he sat down to the table, he wasn't very hungry. His mind kept going over that wretched throw he had made that had spoiled his good catch. Why couldn't he have taken more time and not moved too fast so that his lame leg set him off balance? He had wanted so desperately to have them say, "Hey, Owlie, that was pretty good. Why don't you play outfield?" Not in real games, of course, but just in practice when it didn't count. He could do something to be useful if they'd only give him a chance. He knew he could.

"Don't you want any more pie?" His mother's fingers spelled out the words, and she looked at him anxiously.

Owlie shook his head. "Isn't it time to go to the island, Dad?" he asked.

"Give me a half hour to look at the paper," said

his father. "What do you think you're going to see over there?"

"Just exactly nothing, I suppose," said Owlie. "I wonder why this character wants to hide?"

But his father didn't answer. He had risen from the table and was helping to carry out plates, so Owlie trailed him into the kitchen carrying the milk pitcher.

The sun was low and red behind a bank of clouds as together they loaded the dory with supplies for the island, stowing them well forward and putting the eggs and lighter parcels on top.

Owlie held the seaworthy boat against the dock while his father stepped aboard. Then he untied the painter and leaped lightly in amidships, where he fitted an oar between the thole pins.

He rowed bow and his father rowed stern. Pulling with short even strokes, they set off into the harbor, pointing the prow of the dory toward the island. It was a longer row from their dock than it would have been if they had launched a boat in front of Westerly.

The boy concentrated all his muscles on bending to the rhythm of the strong back in front of him. Lulled by the sound of the dipping oars that thumped against the thole pins and by the water slapping the sides of the boat, all the sore memory of that bad throw faded and gradually died out. He watched the blazing sunset, which meant good weather again tomorrow, and kept to the pace of the stroke as they rowed on in silence, which was finally broken by his father saying:

Red sky at night, sailors' delight.
Red sky at morning, sailors take warning.

"Yes," agreed Owlie, who had heard this before. He turned his head to look at the island growing steadily closer. "It's high tide," he said. "Turtle Rock is covered. This harbor is full of rocks. You sure have to know the channel to get from our place to the island without stoving a hole in your boat."

His father grunted assent and looked over his shoulder to gauge his distance from the landing beach.

Now the writing was clearly visible on the no-trespassing sign, and the boy, again peering over his shoulder, could see a tin box placed beside it. At the sight a thrill of fear made his hands go damp on the oars, as he realized that the man undoubtedly was watching from behind the shelter of the trees. He looked at his father, wondering whether he too felt anxious, but his face was calm and impassive as always.

When the keel of the boat scraped the wet sand Owlie jumped ashore, holding the painter with both hands. He kept the bow steady while his father clambered forward and stepped out. All the time the boy's eyes roved furtively, trying to discover a trace of the stranger, and he was only brought back to the business of the moment by his father's sharp command, "Here, help me pull her up!"

When the dory was safely grounded, they began to unload, mounding the supplies next to the tin box and setting the cans in orderly rows like soldiers.

Aside from the wind humming in the branches of the pine trees and the lapping of the water on the rocks, the silence was oppressive, and Owlie spoke to hear the sound of his own voice. "Lucky it's not raining, or we'd need a tarpaulin. Wet bread wouldn't taste so good to *him*." As he said the word he looked again over his shoulder.

The faint smell of a campfire drifted on the evening air and mingled with the scent of sea-washed rocks, bayberry, and sweet fern. He longed, yet dreaded, to discover the stranger, whose presence was made real by the scent of smoke. His skin began to prickle with the eerie feeling of being watched.

For the first time he was setting foot on the island, which had always beckoned him so mysteriously. The sun had gone below the horizon, and the air felt cool. What little courage he felt began to sink with the oncoming darkness, but still he looked curiously about him, and he saw that a path led from the dry white strip of beach, between gray rocks and on into a cluster of pines and scrub oak. But he was not allowed to linger and look any longer.

Moving with his usual slow composure, his father motioned him into the boat and shoved off. Jumping aboard, he passed beside his son to take his seat in the stern. After the first few strokes to take the dory into deeper water, he held his port oar steady while Owlie pulled with chopping dips of his starboard oar to swing the dory around and head her toward home.

They were a few hundred feet from the island before the boy spoke, and then it was in a low voice. "I didn't see him, did you?"

"Curiosity kills more people than cats, son, or

73

at least loses them their jobs," said his father briefly. "It's a good thing to learn early to mind your own business."

"Why would he want to hide?" asked Owlie.

"I don't know, and I don't care," said his father. "I'm carrying out Dr. Delafield's orders."

"I think the man must be crazy to want to spend a whole summer by himself, not seeing anyone. Weren't you sort of scared on the island?"

"No. I trust the doctor. He knows what he's doing."

For some time they rowed in silence and at last came alongside the dock, where the water lay dark in the dusk that was fading into night. On shore a light shining from the window of the kitchen glowed in welcome. As they walked through the dry sand toward the garden gate, each carrying an oar over his shoulder, they heard the weird night "gwonk" of a bittern in a nearby marsh, and the safe coziness of the house seemed beautiful.

Owlie was tired and went upstairs early. In his room he undressed and put on his pajamas, but before getting into bed, he pulled from a table drawer a magazine clipping that he had read so often the edges were torn. Tonight he looked at it for the hundredth time. It was headed *The Power of Prayer on Plants,* and it went on to say, "Extraordinary experiments have been carried out by a Professor Smedly, who claims to have made plants grow by praying over them each night and morning."

Owlie read no farther. Instead he knelt down by his bed. With his hands folded and eyes closed tightly, he said the prayer that he had repeated every morning and every night for two months. "Dear God, please make me grow taller."

SIX

A week after Dr. Little's visit, the blacksmith arrived. He backed his truck into the driveway and started working the bellows that made the slumbering fire in his forge flare hotly enough to heat iron.

Owlie held Mystery's halter and watched fascinated as the blacksmith, dressed in his heavy leather apron, pared off hunks of old hoof, resting the horse's bent leg against his knee as he worked. Then there was the sound of a hammer ringing on the anvil and tapping out sparks from molten metal as he fitted shoes for Mystery's feet.

When the work was completed the blacksmith straightened up, wiped one heavily muscled arm across his perspiring face, and spoke to Owlie. "Dr. Little sent over a package. He said he could get this stuff wholesale. I was to say he thanked your father for some lobsters he dropped off at his place."

The boy took the proffered package from the man's hand. It was big and bulky. When he unwrapped it, to his amazement he found a complete grooming kit. He picked up a short curved metal object and felt the point with one finger. "What's this?" he asked.

"Hoof pick," answered the blacksmith. "Use it to clean out your horse's feet in case he's picked up a stone. This here's a tail comb. You can make his mane and tail real fancy with this."

Owlie held up a big brush with long stiff bristles and examined it carefully.

"Know how to use it?" asked the blacksmith.

"No," said Owlie.

"Brush your horse thoroughly with that. It's called a dandy brush. Then take this body brush with the shorter bristles. That cleans the skin. When it gets dirty, rub it back and forth on this metal curry comb. Use some elbow grease. Know what that is? You can't buy it at the store." The blacksmith chuckled as he threw his hammer into the truck and closed up the back. "I'll send the bill," he said, and jumping onto the front seat, he drove away in such a hurry that Owlie imagined forty other horses waiting for him.

The boy had understood the man's remark. Elbow grease was the energy in his arms that added to the fine equipment Dr. Little had sent him would make Mystery's coat shine. He set to work with a will, wondering all the time why the vet had been so kind as to give him this wonderful present.

At the end of an hour and a half sweat was pouring down his face, but the horse was beginning to look like a different animal. He decided a cooling ride on the beach would be good for both of them.

Sometimes he used the saddle and sometimes he didn't. Today he decided he would, and he fetched it and the bridle from the stable.

The horse seemed to enjoy any handling, whether it was grooming or shoeing or saddling and bridling. As Dr. Little had said, he had been started right. Having discovered that Owlie was his friend, all the fears that had come from the abuse he had suffered seemed to vanish. He gave himself confidently into his young owner's hands and trusted everything he did.

The boy mounted and patted the bay's neck, which was beginning to show signs of becoming smooth and glossy. He called to Sam, who was lazing in the shade. "Come on, boy, want to go for a ride?"

As soon as they reached the beach the dog

splashed into the water, but when Owlie set off at a brisk trot along the shore, Sam followed at a lumbering lope.

They passed Westerly, where Mystery, out of the gaiety of his newfound health and spirits, tossed his head and shield at the steep flight of steps that descended from the cliff to the sand. But Owlie only laughed. His borrowed saddle fitted him as if it had been made to order, and although he had been riding only a matter of weeks, he rode fairly well so that the horse's sideways steps did not unseat him. The hours he had spent every day on Mystery's back had strengthened his muscles and given him confidence.

Farther up the beach children were playing in the sand with little shovels and pails and were paddling in the water. As the big dog and the horse came in sight mothers gathered the small ones to them. But when Owlie slowed to a walk as he passed, they stood beaming and called to Sam, who wagged his tail and seemed to smile at the children.

"What a picture they make!" he heard one mother say.

Leaning forward, Owlie patted the bay neck in front of him and smoothed the dark mane, confident that the compliment was due to the fine grooming he had just given his horse.

Wanting to show him off, he set out at a canter and after a time disappeared from their sight around a curve in the shoreline.

The wind blew in his face, the horse moved in long rocking strides under him, and he felt as free and happy as the sea gulls that circled overhead in the blue sky.

Sam was being left behind, and Owlie was becoming tired. His lame leg was aching from the grip of his knees on the saddle, and he was about to pull to a stop when suddenly he felt Mystery reach for the bit and saw ahead of him the outline of a large sunken drainage pipe from which the sand had eroded. With a clutch of fear he realized his horse, whose ears were pricked forward and who was increasing his stride with each step, was planning to jump this barrier. Owlie pulled on the reins and tried to stop. But his grip was becoming weak, and he put no authority into his signal.

He could feel the power of the animal under him and his invincible determination to jump. Not being able to stop, Owlie dropped the reins and clutched at the mane just before he felt Mystery leave the ground and soar into the air. It was tremendous! It was like flying; it made him gasp.

But as they landed, his grip on the mane was torn loose, and he fell heavily to the ground. The impact knocked out his wind, and he lay on his back gasping for air.

After a moment he was conscious of Sam's panting face thrust anxiously into his. He moved a little and realized that the sand was soft where he had landed and that he was not hurt. In a moment he sat up and saw Mystery strolling about nearby, reins dangling, nose to the ground, and snuffling to see whether seaweed would taste good.

Very quietly so as not to excite the horse, he rose to his feet and walked slowly toward him, gathered up the reins and patted his neck, feeling apologetic at having fallen off after that splendid jump.

Before mounting, he glanced over his shoulder to be certain that the curve in the shore had hidden him from the view of the children and their mothers.

They rode on about a mile farther with Owlie keeping his eyes open to be sure there wasn't anything ahead that Mystery might consider a jump. As long as he kept him walking or trotting, the

boy had the feeling his horse wouldn't behave as he had just done. It was at a canter and faced with a barrier that some sort of irresistible urge seemed to come over the horse, as it had when he took the four-and-a-half-foot jump out of Mr. Hammond's enclosure.

"You're just a jumping fool," he told him, dropping his face onto Mystery's mane and grabbing him affectionately around the neck. Then he straightened up quickly, wondering whether anyone had seen what he suddenly felt was a sissy way to behave.

It was certainly time to head toward home. Sam was beginning to drag his feet. They had ridden almost to the point where the beach curved round and faced out to the open sea. Off in the distance he could hear the low roar of big waves coming ashore where breakwaters protected the point from the force of the storms. Sometime they would ride that far but not today.

He turned about and headed back, making sure when he passed the long pipe that he kept his horse near the water and walking so that he wouldn't get any ideas. It had been fun to fly through the air as Mystery soared over the jump, but he knew he didn't understand how to sit properly and that he would almost certainly fall off again if he tried it.

The children saw him coming from afar and stood watching as he approached. One little girl in a pink bathing suit whose tightly-braided pigtails stood out from her head like small bow-tied ropes looked solemnly at him as he passed and said, "You've been playing in the sand. Your back's all sandy."

Owlie gave her a cold stare, but Sam in passing bumped the child affectionately with his huge head which made her sit down hard and begin to howl. Her mother picked her up and kissed her. "The nice doggy didn't mean it, Rosie," she said.

Owlie rode past Westerly at a trot. Keeping his head turned toward the island, he let his thoughts of the stranger run unhindered.

"He's a loony, I'll bet," he said to himself. "Maybe he climbs up one of those trees like a monkey and watches when we unload the boat. Someday maybe he'll pick up a rock and throw it at Dad and knock him out, and there I'll be all alone with him."

Safe on shore, the thought gave him an almost pleasurable thrill of excitement as he imagined himself dragging his father to the boat, heaving him in, and rowing away under a shower of stones.

Remembering he must come to a walk so as to bring the horse in cool, he pulled lightly on the reins and felt Mystery respond at once by slowing his pace. Easy and relaxed the boy's back swayed to the horse's long stride. The sweat began to dry under his shirt. He started to itch and thought with pleasure of a swim.

On a loose rein they rode up to the stable door, where he dismounted. Leading Mystery into the stall, he unsaddled him, rubbed him down with a cloth, picked out his feet with the hoof pick, checked the water bucket, and forked some hay into a corner.

His mother was ironing in the kitchen and looked up with a smile as he entered. "Did you have a nice ride?" she questioned with quick fingers.

Owlie nodded. He had remembered to brush the sand off his back before going in the house.

"Why don't you ask some of your classmates down to swim sometime?" his mother spelled out, giving him a kind and anxious look. "I could make some nice sandwiches they would enjoy, or you could have them for lunch if you wanted to."

A tender feeling of gratitude and pity surged up in the boy and collided inside him with another feeling, one of resentment, as he pictured the rude stares some of the boys would give his mother.

Not all of them, not Roy Bladen for instance. But Roy wouldn't want to come down to swim. He had all the gang to play ball with, and afterward they always went together and swam at the public beach.

Owlie gave one of his crooked smiles out of the corner of his mouth. "Thanks, Mom," he spelled. "I'm too busy."

She motioned toward the wastepaper basket, which it was his job to empty.

"Okay," he agreed, and picking it up, he went outside and dumped it into a big barrel.

That night at supper his father said, "I'm planning to drive your mother over to Aunt Julia's to visit for a night the first week in August. I've been trying to figure out what you could do with your horse if you went along."

"Can't I stay here?" asked Owlie. "I'd rather ride than sit around at Aunt Julia's."

His father frowned and considered the question. "Well," he said at last, "I don't know why not."

Excitement showed on Owlie's face. To be left alone and in charge of the house! He liked the idea. "I won't be lonely," he said. "I have my paper route every morning, and I'll ride Mystery and I'll have Sam."

"I kind of hate to go," said his father. "I have

the funniest feeling that somebody has been prowling around inside the house at Westerly. Everything's always locked when I go up in the morning. Nothing's missing. At least I'm not sure. I could swear there once were four books lying on the living-room table. Now there are two. I must be imagining it because I've checked every window, and they're not only locked but the shutters are closed and nailed shut."

"You need a vacation," said Owlie.

SEVEN

The seventh of August was hot, even for that time of year. Owlie hoped his mother and father were enjoying themselves at Aunt Julia's, but in the town where she lived he was willing to bet it was a lot hotter than by the sea. He was glad he hadn't accompanied them on their visit. Just the same, as the afternoon wore on he began to have a rather lonesome feeling.

At suppertime he went to the refrigerator and found a piece of cold chicken, some carrot sticks, and a slice of chocolate cake his mother had left for him. These he carried, along with a glass of milk, to the end of the dock, where he sat on the edge dangling his bare feet in the water.

Sam sat down beside him and looked out toward the sea. He panted with his mouth wide open, but every once in awhile he pulled in his pink tongue and swallowed before opening his mouth to begin again the dripping and the heavy breathing that are a dog's way of perspiring.

"Gosh, Sam, but you're hot. It's that big fur coat you're wearing," said Owlie, who was dressed only in shorts, his brown chest exposed to what little breeze there was.

"I'll bet it's cooler right out on the water. You could get in the skiff with me if you'd sit still.

He scrambled to his feet and walked back to the beach where the boat was pulled well up onto the sand. Untying the painter from the anchor rope, he pushed the light boat into the water. "Come on, Sam," he called. "Come on, get in," and he patted the seat in the stern to show what he meant. The dog obeyed. His immense bulk filled half the boat, but at the word of command he sat down uncomfortably and stared at Owlie, who was climbing aboard.

The boy unshipped the oars and put them in the oarlocks. With short strokes he began to row along the shoreline, watching with some amusement the big dog's efforts to keep his balance. It would have been highly dangerous to go far out with an overloaded boat and an unsteady dog. He realized that. But he didn't intend to go more than a few yards away from the beach.

In the back of his mind something told him

that he knew perfectly well his father wouldn't have approved of what he was doing. "What could happen?" he reasoned. "If we tip over, I'll just wade ashore and pull the boat in. It's not more than up to my waist here."

The tide was going out and the comparatively narrow neck of the harbor gave it a strong pull, so Owlie rowed harder with his port oar than with his starboard oar to keep even with the shoreline.

They were nearing Westerly. He looked over his shoulder and wondered how many gray wooden steps there were in that long flight that led to the cliff. A path steep enough for a goat went up a few yards away through a tangle of wild white-rose bushes.

Turning his head, he stared at the island and speculated again on its weird inhabitant, who had run up the flag again four days ago wanting more supplies—sardines, notebooks, pencils, and more bread. Owlie had forgotten now all the things that had been on the list, but there were at least fifty items, including the tins of fruit that he had helped unload beside the no-trespassing sign. What thoughts would a loony want to write down in a notebook, he wondered.

The heat of the sun had gone as it sank lower

and lower. Owlie even began to feel chilly with no shirt on. Sam had stopped panting, but he looked very unhappy balancing his great weight in the stern with his tail and hindquarters on the seat and his paws in the bottom of the boat. His eyes had a reproachful and beseeching look.

"Let's go home," said Owlie, and he pulled hard on the starboard oar to turn around.

The sudden change of course made Sam lurch and almost lose his balance. Owlie let go the oars to steady the boat, which had nearly upset. They had shipped some water, and the boy felt an uneasy twinge of anxiety.

He reached again for the oars to start rowing, realizing that while looking at the island he had gone off course and was farther out than he had intended. The port oar was resting in the oarlock and dragging in the water, but when he felt for the starboard oar, there was nothing there. He looked down and saw to his horror that it was drifting rapidly away from him on the outgoing tide.

He didn't know what to do. If Sam hadn't been aboard, he would have gone to the stern and tried to paddle with his remaining oar. If he paddled in the bow he would only go round and round.

When the thought occurred to him to abandon

the boat and swim for the shore, they had already drifted so far out he didn't dare chance it. "Stay with your boat" had always been the instruction his father had given him.

Perhaps someone would see him. He looked toward the deserted beach where yesterday the children and their mothers had been sunning on the sand. Oh, if it were only bright daylight! Long ago people had gone in to supper. Children would be tucked in bed now, their parents at the movies perhaps, or maybe reading books by some safe cozy lamp.

Darkness was coming on apace, and still they drifted away on the outgoing tide.

Turtle Rock lay ahead, its humped outline like the shell of a tortoise becoming more visible as the water receded.

Sudden terror clutched at the boy's heart, for he saw that they were drifting toward the island and the rocks and shoals that surrounded it.

But what if he managed by poling with his oar in the shallows to miss grounding near the island —would the current of the tide pull them through the neck of the harbor and out to sea? Before that happened surely somebody would notice him. Or would they? It was getting darker every moment.

He would shout as they passed the lighthouse at the point. Surely someone would hear him there. He looked at Sam's discouraged face. The dog's ears were drooping and his eyes were full of reproach.

Owlie lost all sense of what was possible and in his determination to stay away from the island, he turned around in the boat and began paddling from the bow seat. But his efforts only brought the skiff broadside to the tide, and they drifted on as fast as ever.

The island was looming nearer and nearer; its rocks and dark pine trees threatened him with their secret. Turtle Rock lay ahead.

Almost frantic with fear Owlie stood up in the boat, which teetered dangerously. As they approached the rock he reached with the oar to fend it off, but his sudden movement unseated Sam, who gave a lurch and then a scrabble of his great paws.

Desperately the boy tried to get the skiff in balance by shifting his weight, but it was too late. They overturned with a clatter of the oar striking the boat, the splash of Sam's bulk hitting the water, and the sickening sound of Owlie's head striking the rock.

Sam began to swim and turned his head looking

for his master, who floated without movement near him. There was a desperate look in the dog's eyes, but the inherited lore of a hundred generations of ancestors that had lived on the rocky coast of northern Newfoundland awoke the rescue instinct.

Owlie lay floating on his back. Paddling mightily, the dog grabbed one of the boy's arms in his great jaws, as if it were a stick he was retrieving, and set out for the island only a short distance away.

When they came to the shallows and Sam could no longer swim, he grabbed Owlie by the seat of his pants and pulled and tugged, walking backward toward dry land, where he finally let go of his burden on the beach and shook himself.

The dusk was deepening. The flowing tide slapped ripples against the rocks, and a breeze coming in off the sea seemed to sigh of loneliness and of night.

Out of the shadow of the pines a figure slowly emerged and walked toward the boy and the dog. Sam saw it and raised his head defiantly to defend his master. His eyes, ordinarily kind, blazed with ferocity, and a low growl warned the man not to approach a step farther.

The figure stopped. Owlie stirred but he didn't

open his eyes. One weak arm lifted toward the dog's neck, then flopped back on the sand.

Very low, inaudible except to the dog, the figure spoke. "Sam," it said.

Suddenly the dog's eyes were alight with confidence and joy, and his tail beat the air in a rapture of recognition.

Assured but unhurried, the man approached the boy and bent over him feeling his pulse and moving his legs and arms gently.

With a groan and a convulsive jerk, Owlie opened his eyes suddenly and looked up into a face so terrible he fainted.

EIGHT

When consciousness returned, he found himself in semidarkness within a small room. An oil lamp on a table beside the camp bed, where he lay, made a pool of yellow light and sent black shadows crawling up the walls.

He turned his head, which felt sore, while he tried to remember what had happened and what terror lurked in his mind.

A deep voice that seemed to have been going on for some time kept speaking in low soothing tones. But although he moved his head still farther, there was no one to be seen.

"Owlie," said the voice, "you're all right. Everything's all right. There's nothing to be afraid of."

The sound of the voice was familiar. He thought that it came from behind a door that he could see at the end of the room.

"I must get up," said Owlie drowsily. "I have to deliver the papers."

97

"Lie still a little longer," said the voice. "You bumped your head on a rock, and Sam dragged you ashore. But you're all right. Your boat's safe; I pulled it up on the beach. I found your glasses on the sand. They're on the table beside you."

"Who are you?" asked Owlie. "Where am I?"

"You're on Hideaway Island," said the voice. "Tomorrow you can row back. I'll lend you an oar. Will your family worry about you?"

"They're away—they won't worry," said Owlie. He propped himself up on an elbow and looked about. The walls, made of weathered boards, were decorated with old maps and unframed pictures of sailing ships. A rough bookshelf full of books faced him from beside an uncurtained window through which he could see moonlight and the dark branches of pine trees. In the center of the room two wooden chairs stood by a table, where the remains of a supper were spread. Beside him on a low table he saw a glass of water, which he reached for and drank with thirsty gulps.

The voice continued to soothe him but a great black shadow was jumping threateningly on the wall, and he shrank down in fright until he realized that it was his own arm moving in front of the lamp.

"Why don't you come out? Who are you?" asked the boy. He looked into a dark corner and saw that the heap of blackness there was Sam, curled up and sound asleep. At least his dog wasn't afraid.

"Owlie, I don't come out because I would frighten you. My face has been scarred by fire."

Scarred by fire! A girl in a burning hospital saved by—

"Dr. Delafield!" cried Owlie. "Is it you?"

"Yes, Owlie. I'm sorry I gave you a shock. My bone and skin grafts still look pretty raw. I came here because I love the sea. I was sick of being in a hospital. I know my face is pretty upsetting to people, and that's why I'm staying away from them. I thought if I could smell salt water and seaweed and hear gulls and listen to the sound of waves, it would cheer me up."

"Yes," said Owlie. He remembered the tight angry feeling he had experienced after his encounter with Bud Dover's father and how it had all floated away as he swam in the sea. More recently, after that clumsy throw that had made such a fool of him, the sound of water against the dory and the smell of the sea had made him feel all right again as he rowed the supplies to the island with his father. He understood what the doctor meant. But he didn't say anything. The sudden memory of a nightmare face that had appeared for one terrible moment before blackness closed over him prevented him from speaking. Without moving, he listened to the man's voice, which went on in low calm tones.

"A burning timber knocked me down and shattered my jaw. At first they thought the heat had affected my eyes and that I'd never see again. But thank God they're all right. I can read—I'm fortunate."

Fortunate! thought Owlie. When his face is so scarred he is afraid of frightening people.

The doctor's voice continued cheerfully. "It won't always be as bad as this. I'll have more plastic surgery done later, and the red of the scars will fade. They're allowing me a little holiday to recover from the beauty treatment they've already given me." The voice took on a stern quality. "Now I want you to go to sleep. Tomorrow around noon the tide will be low enough, and you are to row home following the course I am about to describe to you. Stand in front of the no-trespassing sign and take a sight on the flagpole at Westerly, then row straight toward it. There is a sand bar that extends from the island to the shore like a path. Until your head feels perfectly all right I don't want you tipping over in deep water and having to swim. It will be shallow if you keep to the sand bar. Sam can follow along behind. He'll be all right. You should have known enough, Owlie, not to take a big dog like that in a boat with you."

"Yes," agreed the boy. "What do you do all day?" he asked, hoping he wasn't being too inquisitive.

"I'm writing medical articles. I want to be by myself just now, but I must say, Owlie, I've enjoyed talking to you."

"People are going to be awfully mad if I don't deliver the papers tomorrow morning," said Owlie.

"They'll live through it for once. Tell them you were unavoidably detained. Do you still ride that bike you had last year?"

"Yes, but I have a horse too. I'm going to deliver papers on him pretty soon. His leg's all right now He won't have any breakfast if I don't go home." Owlie's voice sounded troubled.

"A horse! What's his name?"

"Mystery. And boy, can he jump!"

"Is that so? I've done a lot of riding. I'd like to see your horse someday."

"Oh, he's a nice horse. I began riding him bareback."

"You did? When I was a boy we used to ride bareback. Sometimes we rode two on a horse."

Owlie was becoming drowsy; the doctor's voice

was fading away into the distance. He heard him say, "Don't look for me in the morning. You'll find some sandwiches down by the boat. When the tide's low enough so you can see all of Turtle Rock, it will be time for you to start. Bring back the oar I'm lending you next time you row over with your father."

"I wouldn't be scared to see you now, Dr. Delafield," murmured Owlie.

The night wind sighed and the boy slept, his face turned toward the wall. In the corner Sam snored, and out under the stars a figure wrapped in a sleeping bag passed the night lying on the ground.

It was late morning when Owlie awoke. He stirred, opened his eyes, and looked in the corner for Sam, who wasn't there. The door of the shack was open, and the boy guessed the dog must have gone for a walk around the island.

With a careful hand he touched the bump on his head, which was still sore. But when he sat up and got to his feet, he felt as well as usual except for a slight throbbing around his temples. He reached for his glasses and found them on the table by his bed.

Obeying the doctor's instructions not to try to see him, he walked down a path that led from the shack, where he had spent the night. On his left a clear spring bubbled out of a hollow in the ground, and he knelt down and drank deeply. The water refreshed him, but he felt hungry.

On the strip of beach by the no-trespassing sign he saw his skiff pulled up and Sam sitting beside it.

"You want to go home, boy, don't you? Well, you can't just now." Owlie looked toward Turtle Rock, which was not yet entirely out of water. In the distance, high on the cliff, he could see the gilt ball on top of the flagpole at Westerly and remembered that by that sign he was to set his course.

He peered inside the skiff. The lone oar with which he had struggled so frustratingly the evening before lay there, and beside it was another one that did not quite match in size and length. Lying on the seat in the stern was a packet of sandwiches, a bottle of ginger ale, and an opener.

Owlie sat down on the sand. The ginger ale was warm, but it tasted good. He tipped the bottle up and drank the last drop, then opened the paper packet and ate four ham sandwiches after first offering one to Sam, who sniffed and rejected it. Apparently the dog and the doctor had had a good breakfast together while Owlie slept.

For a little while he lay on his back and watched

the stormy-looking clouds that were building up in the sky. Idly he sifted sand through his fingers and thought about what he would like to be when he became a man. He was sure he wanted to go to college and be a doctor. But it would be expensive to go to college and medical school too. Maybe he'd never make it. Presently he sat up and saw that Turtle Rock was high and dry, lying there like a great tortoise sunning itself with head and tail tucked in under its shell.

"Come on, Sam," said Owlie, and he pushed the skiff into the water. "You've got to walk and swim, boy, I'm not going to take you in any boat again."

As he pulled toward the shore he understood what the doctor had meant. If he kept the no-trespassing sign in line with the stern of his skiff, and the flagpole in line with the bow, he was on the right course. It surprised him to see how little Sam had to swim. He had never known about this bar that extended just like a path from the island to Westerly.

A few yards off shore he turned the bow of the boat in the direction of home and followed the shoreline, rowing with strong strokes to get back to his horse, while Sam trotted along the beach, keeping abreast of him.

His head had begun to ache a little, but aside from that he felt fine. Some unanswered questions were going through his mind. How had the doctor gotten to the island all the way from Chicago? What did he expect to do, live on the island always? Perhaps he was wondering who would want him for a doctor with a face that scared people.

When Owlie saw their dock ahead of him and the gray house covered with roses, he felt as if he had been gone from home a long time. Everything looked familiar and wonderful but just a little lonesome without his family.

NINE

Mystery received special attention during the day
to make up for having eaten no breakfast. He was
given additional oats and a grooming that made
his coat shine. He had greeted Owlie's return with
whinnies and had buried his nose in the water
bucket the boy filled to the brim. "Poor Mystery,"
said Owlie. "Did you think I'd deserted you?"

Along about midafternoon he had an inspiration.
Perhaps no one had picked up his New York papers,
and he could still deliver them. The idea of his bike
bored him. Besides, Mystery needed exercise.

He saddled his horse and trotted along the path
to the village with Sam tagging in the rear.

The usual ball game was in progress, and as he
skirted the edge of the field at a canter, he heard
Roy Bladen shout, "Hey look, it's Owlie," and the
whole game came to a stop while everyone gaped
as he passed.

At the village store which carried newspapers, he dismounted and wondered what to do with his horse. Fortunately the man inside had heard the clatter of his arrival and came to the door in shirt sleeves. "Where were you this morning?" he asked.

"I was unavoidably detained," said Owlie, using the doctor's words. "Has everyone picked up their papers?"

"Only Mr. FitzGibbons. He was mad as a hop-toad."

"I'll deliver them now," said Owlie. Then his face went blank as he tried to think how he could carry them. There was no convenient basket fixed to Mystery's neck such as he had on his bicycle. Why hadn't he thought of that before? His head still ached. Maybe that was why he was so stupid.

But when the man returned he was carrying the papers in a canvas bag with a shoulder strap attached.

"Hold it till I mount, will you?" asked Owlie.

He settled himself in the saddle and slung the heavy bag onto his shoulder. "Thanks," he said. "I won't be late again." With a gentle pressure of his legs he started his horse moving at a walk through the village, where the clipping and clopping of four shod feet made such a tattoo that people came to shop windows to see him pass and automobiles gave him the right of way.

When his customers saw him ride up astride a horse, most of them were too surprised to remember to complain. To each Owlie said, "I am sorry I was unavoidably detained." His explanation for the most part was accepted with a polite smile, but one man said grumpily, "I trust this won't happen again."

It always seemed funny to Owlie that grown-up men got into an awful state when they didn't receive a newspaper right on time. Often enough he had heard from his customers that the boy who had delivered the papers before him was impossible, sometimes a whole hour late and twice he hadn't come at all. He himself had built up a good business by being regular and prompt.

His bag was becoming lighter. They trotted along on the edge of Seacoast Road, stopping at about every third house.

He decided it was much more fun delivering his papers from his horse than from his bike. When he turned in at the last summer cottage he saw a girl sitting in a rocking chair, knitting, so he rode right up to the porch instead of throwing the paper over the railing.

At the sight of Mystery the girl put down her work and got up with an exclamation of surprise. "Oh, he's beautiful," she cried, "just the color of a peeled horse chestnut. His mane and tail are dark as smoke."

Owlie smiled at her.

Mystery appeared to enjoy her flattering voice and before the boy could stop him, he had moved up two steps of the porch with his forelegs and stretched out his neck in her direction.

"He's sweet!" she cried. "May I give him a lump of sugar?"

"Just today," conceded Owlie. "Too much sugar isn't good for him."

The girl ran into the house and returned with a large-sized sugar lump, which Mystery took delicately from her hand.

"What would you rather I give him next time?" she asked.

"A piece of an apple would be better," said Owlie, who was smoothing his horse's mane proudly.

"May I give your big black dog a cookie?" she asked, moving to take one from a plate on the table beside her rocking chair.

"I don't think he'd eat it," said Owlie. "He likes meat."

However, after a disdainful sniff Sam condescended to take the cookie in his great jaws and swallowed it with one solemn gulp.

"See you tomorrow," said the girl. "I just *love* your horse and your dog."

Feeling a new assurance, Owlie rode slowly back past the ball field. For once in his life he experienced the sensation of being taller than his schoolmates.

"Hey, Owlie, give us a ride," called Red Wilson.

"Yeah, give us a ride," echoed Roy.

"Don't lose your glasses," shouted Bud Dover.

Owlie responded with a grin that spread right across his face.

Just the same, as he rode on toward home a bitter thought which he had often had before again crossed his mind. They never want me to do anything with them. Desperately he craved to belong to the gang, and they just seemed to take it for granted that he was an outsider; that is, until they needed some help with their homework.

In the driveway by the garage the old station wagon was being unloaded. His parents were back, and his father was pulling out a suitcase while his mother collected coats from the rear seat.

Happy smiles spread over their faces at the sight

111

of their son, mounted on Mystery, looking well and very much alive. His mother also gave the gray house with its roses a loving look, as if she had thought it might have blown away in her absence. They acted, Owlie decided, as if they had been gone a whole week instead of just two days and a night, and so did Sam, who circled round them, barking his welcome home.

"Everything all right?" asked his father.

"Sure," said Owlie.

"You didn't see anyone prowling around Westerly?" asked his father anxiously.

"No," answered the boy. "I haven't been up to Westerly."

"What have you been doing?" asked his father.

"Oh, nothing much," said Owlie. He hadn't yet decided whether to tell his mother and father who the mysterious stranger on the island was. For one thing, he knew he had behaved like a fool taking Sam along in the boat, and he hated to admit his stupidity unless he had to. Furthermore, he enjoyed the idea of a secret between Dr. Delafield and himself.

But when he went upstairs that night and jumped into bed after saying his growing prayer, he began to think about things. That oar he had borrowed from Dr. Delafield must be returned, and he would have to tell his father how he had lost his own. Next time the red flag went up on the island and they took over supplies, he would have to confess how stupid he had been. Even before that his father, who didn't miss much, might notice that the oars in the skiff were of a different size.

The wind was rising and through his wide-open window the boy could hear waves slapping at the dock and coming ashore in regular bursts of sighing and receding water. The harbor would be rough tomorrow but not as rough as out beyond the point on the open ocean where great rollers would crash against the breakwaters.

Between sleeping and waking he lay on his back with his arms at his sides. He heard his mother and father come up the stairs to bed, then close their door.

Sam slept in the hall with his head hanging down over the top step, a position he had decided on as a puppy and which he took up every night. The thump of his big frame settling down on the bare painted floor always gave Owlie a cozy feeling of protection. Tonight he heard Sam sigh deeply as if he intended to sleep the sleep of the just and the overexercised. It had been a rough couple of days

113

for Sam and for Owlie too. And poor Mystery with no breakfast and no water!

The boy's mind strayed to the island, where he pictured the doctor sleeping alone in his shack among the wind-tossed pines with the sound of waves beating on the rocks. It seemed such a dreadful thing that Dr. Delafield, who was loved by everyone in the village, felt he must keep isolated just because his face was terribly broken and scarred. Sam hadn't cared how he looked. He knew that inside he was just the same kind doctor, whose thoughts were the same, whose voice was the same. A dog was wiser than a boy, who couldn't get beyond the way a person looked on the outside. Owlie knew now how silly he had been to let his imagination race on about a madman living on the island. Certainly it had been that idea that had scared him half out of his wits, as well as the sight of that misshapen face with the great red welts of scars staring down at him in the dusk. If he ever saw the doctor again he would have more sense— he hoped.

TEN

It was his father's voice that woke Owlie.

"Son, help me!"

The boy sprang out of bed and opened his door. A draft blew the curtains away from the window, and the boy shivered as he stepped into the hall. The door banged shut behind him.

Sam stood bewilderedly at the top of the stairs, his head turned toward the sound of the agitated voice calling, "Hurry, son, help me!"

Owlie sprang across the hall and through the open door into his parents' bedroom. In the middle of the floor, beyond the big double bed, his father was bending over a heap of white nightgown from which emerged his mother's pale face, twisted in pain.

The only light in the room was a bedside lamp, but Owlie could see that she was lying in an unnatural position.

"She's broken her shoulder," said his father in a tone of agonized pity. "She got up to close the window and tripped over a stool. She didn't turn on the light for fear of waking me. Call the doctor. You'll have to call Beachport; our doctor left the village last night. His father's sick."

Owlie had bent low over his mother and with a gentle hand he touched her cheek in sympathy. She tried a smile in response, but her face tore at his heart.

The telephone was downstairs. He straightened up and hurried toward the hall, clutching at his slipping pajamas, his bare feet scuffing the cold boards of the floor.

The house was chilly from the storm that was blowing outside, and his teeth chattered with cold and nervousness as he lifted the receiver to dial the operator. But when he put the receiver to his ear there was no sound at all, only a terrible blank stillness. The line was dead.

Desperately he jiggled the telephone up and down and tried again—but with the same result.

Apparently the wind that was blowing so strongly had knocked down a wire. There was nothing to do but go upstairs and report the bad news.

From the door he beckoned to his father and in low tones explained the situation.

116

"I'll have to drive to Beachport," said Mr. Jennings, but his voice was grim. "Suppose the doctor's not in when I get there? I can't bear to leave her. Maybe you could ride up to the village and try to call from someone's house. If only it's not the line from the village that's dead."

"I'll go!" cried Owlie. "I'll get a doctor. You stay with Mom."

Brushing past Sam, he limped into his room and quickly put on his blue jeans, sneakers, and a sweat shirt. Down the stairs he ran and snatched a short slicker off a hook in the hall. Clumsily he buttoned it up to his throat while fighting his way through the wind and the darkness to the stable. As he opened the door he heard a rustling and saw Mystery move in the deep straw to face him.

The memory of his mother's agonized face lent speed to the fingers that slid the bit into the horse's mouth and fitted the bridle over his ears. To save time he skipped putting on the saddle.

His breath was coming in short nervous gasps as he led Mystery out into the night. At the feel of the cold wind coming off the sea, the horse flung up his head, pricked his ears, and looked about. The dark cloud of his mane and tail blew like flags, and he shivered a little, catching the boy's excitement.

With a leap Owlie flung himself astride the horse and gathered the reins in his hands while with his legs he gave the signal to go. At a gallop they tore up the lane till they reached the first house, which was the Dovers'. Here he sprang to the ground, and looping the reins over his arm, he led Mystery to the door on which he pounded with his doubled-up fist until it was opened a crack by Bud.

"What's the matter?" he asked crossly.

"Mom's hurt!" cried Owlie. "Call the doctor in Beachport—Dr. Smith's away." All enmity toward Bud had vanished. Here was a human being who could help him. The urgency of his demand seemed to impress Bud, for he turned to the telephone in the hall and took off the receiver.

After a moment he turned around and said, "No one answers; the line's dead."

"Oh!" cried Owlie in despair. "It's the main line then. No one in the village will have a telephone."

Bud stood staring at him stupidly, sheltering himself from the wind behind the half-closed door.

"Never mind," cried Owlie. A sudden resolve had burst in his brain like the sunrise that was beginning to show with a faint glow of pink in the east. The path for him was suddenly plain. Dr. Delafield— the island! He sprang again onto Mystery's bare

118

back, and the horse, catching fire from the boy's trembling excitement, shot like an arrow down the lane and onto the beach.

Owlie crouched low on the outstretched neck, and the sand flew in spurts behind the thudding hoofs as they tore down the shore at a full gallop.

In front of Westerly he pulled to a stop and looked up at the flagpole to get his bearings. Then with an impulsive pull on the reins he turned his horse and splashed into the sea, heading toward the island.

He blessed the hours he had spent keeping Mystery in the water to cure his leg, for the animal was quite unafraid of the spray that enveloped them as they trotted out onto the sandy bar that lay concealed beneath the water.

The tide was fairly high and the going became more difficult. Every few steps Mystery seemed to be swimming. If it hadn't been for the thought of his mother, the boy would have given up and turned back. But the thought of her in pain made him drive his horse forward.

Now in the gradually fading darkness he could see the sign on the beach which gave him his bearings, and with voice and legs he urged his horse on to greater efforts.

The wind whipped the mane into his face, the spray flew as high as his head, and then for a few breathless seconds they were really swimming hard.

Clinging to the horse's mane, half floating, he prayed. "God give Mystery strength to get there." Desperately he stared ahead at the island, where the strong green pine trees anchored in the rocky soil had a look of safety.

All at once the horse found his feet on the sand bar. Head held high, his wet coat glistening, he floundered through the last stretch of deep water and trotted, splashing through the shallows to the shore.

Without pausing, Owlie pressed Mystery forward over the rocks and along the path leading to the shack. Even before he reached it he was calling. "Dr. Delafield! Dr. Delafield!"

The door of the shack swung open and revealed the man looking resentful and startled. Owlie saw the disfigurement of his shattered, scarred face, but now the doctor seemed like an angel from heaven.

"Mom's broken her shoulder," he gasped. "Come."

The doctor stepped calmly into the rosy light of the dawn. "Owlie," he said, "how can I? You took the oar. I have only one." His distorted mouth, pulled down at the corner, enunciated the words with difficulty.

"You've got to come!" cried Owlie, almost sobbing. "She hurts so much. You've got to."

There was a moment's silence; only the boy's heavy breathing could be heard.

"I suppose we can ride two on a horse," said the doctor. "Wait, I'll come."

He went inside the shack and stepped out a few moments later, wearing a pair of old trousers and a turtleneck sweater that he turned up to the line of his jaw.

"Jump off while I mount!" he ordered. "I'll get on first."

The boy obediently slid to the ground and was surprised to see with what agility the doctor sprang astride, using a rock as a mounting block.

"I'll move back onto his rump while you scramble aboard in front of me," said Dr. Delafield. "This is a remarkable horse—he stands so still," he added a moment afterward, for Owlie had managed to wriggle onto the horse's neck and slide backward behind the withers without his taking a step.

"Yes, he is." Owlie was fumbling in his pocket and pulled out a piece of sugar that he thrust at the horse's head, which was turned back expectantly toward him. In his haste the boy almost dropped the reward for good behavior, but Mystery,

with a quick nibble, caught the lump as it slid to the end of Owlic's fingers. "Come on!" he cried. "Let's go."

Headed for home, Mystery plunged bravely into the water, carrying his double load. Encouraged by the boy's voice and his familiar hands on the reins, he strove boldly in the choppy water, where waves struck at him and forced his head high.

The doctor seldom spoke. With one arm he encircled Owlie's waist to steady himself. Occasionally he muttered, "Good boy," or "Good horse." But for the few seconds when they were almost completely submerged, and Mystery was swimming for his life, the doctor was silent. He hung on firmly to the boy, who stayed with the horse by clutching his mane. Confidence seemed to flow through the horse, the boy, and the man. Each believed in the others.

Never for a moment did Owlie's attention waver. He kept his eyes fixed on the flagpole at Westerly and guided his horse's course, while saying over and over, "Come on, that's a good fellow. You can do it."

When at last they splashed ashore in the shallows, the boy felt a sense of triumph and gratitude that made him lean low on his horse's neck and squeeze it quickly with both his arms.

"Stop by the steps," said the doctor. "I'll run up

and get my bag." He slid to the ground and ran up the gray wooden boards, leaving wet marks behind him.

The wind was chilly. Owlie dismounted, and holding the reins, kept Mystery walking up and down at the edge of the waves until he saw the doctor running lightly down the steps, carrying his black bag.

Again the horse seemed to sense the importance of the moment. He stood perfectly still while the man and the boy both managed to clamber to his back.

"Can you stay on if we canter?" asked Owlie.

"Sure," said the doctor. "I told you I used to do this when I was a boy."

"How did you get in the house?" asked Owlie.

"My key. Until I gave you my oar, I used to row over in the middle of the night and take books back to the island." His voice sounded jiggly. "Not as young as I was," he panted. "Bareback riding's for the young."

"Shall I slow up?" asked Owlie.

"No, no, I'm all right. We're nearly there, and this is a good way to dry off," said the doctor, who was holding onto Owlie with one hand and his black bag with the other.

As they neared the little gray house with the

roses, a troubling thought crossed the boy's mind. He felt he should prepare his mother and father so that they wouldn't show horror at the doctor's appearance, as Owlie himself had done that first night he saw the scarred face.

"Whoa," he said as he drew up at the gate. "Dr. Delafield, will you hold Mystery? I want to tell them you're here."

Sam greeted him at the front door, but Owlie brushed past him and limped rapidly up the stairs.

His mother was moaning softly—terrible, inarticulate moans, like an animal. How awful not to be able to speak and say how it hurt! There was something so different about her as she lay there covered by a blanket, which his father had pulled off the bed. Owlie wanted her back in the kitchen, smiling, feeding the canary, baking cookies. She wasn't the mother he knew. She made him afraid.

"Dad," he said. "Dr. Delafield's here. Don't let him see you think his face looks awful. It's him. Don't forget it's him. Tell Mom. I'll go get him."

Without waiting for another word, he dashed down the stairs and out of the house.

The doctor turned his kind eyes on Owlie. "All right?" he asked, and the boy knew he understood why it had been necessary to wait before going in.

"Yes," said Owlie. He suddenly realized that one

of the best doctors in Chicago, perhaps one of the best doctors in the whole country, was going in to help his mother, and his heart felt light.

He led Mystery into the stable and rubbed him down well with wisps of straw and then a cloth. This morning he truly loved his horse. Heretofore he had liked him, enjoyed riding him, wanted him to be comfortable and happy. But now a feeling welled up in Owlie's heart that made him want to caress the shiny bay neck, stroke the wiry mane, and tell him over and over again, "Mystery, you were wonderful, so bold, so brave, and you stood still while we mounted. I think you're the nicest horse in the whole world."

With a lavish hand he filled the measure with grain and emptied it into the feed box in the stall. While he forked in sweet-smelling hay he listened to the happy munching of Mystery eating, and he remembered the poor sad horse he had bought for forty dollars. It was hard to believe that these glossy rounded sides had once shown every rib. Or that the happy, confident eyes the horse turned on him had been filled with fear as he had limped away from Mr. Hammond toward the few sprigs of clover offered over the fence.

"I love you, Mystery," said Owlie.

ELEVEN

"She's resting comfortably," said the doctor as he came through the kitchen door to join Owlie and his father, who were sitting at the table under the canary's cage.

"Let me get you some bacon and eggs. You make more toast, son. Here's a cup of coffee, Doctor." Thomas Jennings pulled out a chair and seated Dr. Delafield at the table, then went to the stove and dished up two fried eggs and a few pieces of crisp bacon.

"Thank you," said the doctor. "I gave her a shot of morphine to stop the pain. The shoulder's going to be all right. It was dislocated, not broken."

"My wife would have been in pain for hours if you hadn't come. How can I ever thank you," said Mr. Jennings.

Owlie broke rapidly into the conversation. He was embarrassed by a strange look on his father's face and the moisture in his eyes. "It was Dr. Delafield who took the books. He took his own books. He rowed over in the night."

"I'm relieved," said his father. "I *thought* some books were missing from a table." As he talked he was trying to look, but not appear to look, at the doctor's scarred face. Owlie could see him gradually getting used to it, as he himself had done.

The canary bounced from perch to perch over their heads, swinging his cage and spilling seed. "You put too much in his cup," said Owlie. "Mom only fills it halfway." He absentmindedly swept the scattered seeds into his hand. Somehow nothing looked as nice with his mother sick. The plates on the table didn't match; the eggs had stuck in the pan.

"Have some more toast," Thomas Jennings urged the doctor. "Son, pour a little more coffee."

"No, thank you; it was very good." Dr. Delafield pushed away his empty plate. "Now if I could trouble you to row me back to Hideaway Island."

Thomas Jennings glanced out the window. "We'd better take the dory," he said. "The harbor's pretty rough this morning."

"The doctor lent me an oar," said Owlie sheepishly. "You'd better take it back."

"I noticed the oars in the skiff didn't match. I meant to ask you about that," said his father.

"I tipped over—Sam tipped over. We spent the night on the island. That's how I knew the doctor was there."

His father's keen look seemed to say, Never mind. You can tell me more later.

Dr. Delafield stood up. "Owlie, now that you know about the sand bar that leads to the island, you'd better come over and call on me again with that remarkable horse of yours. I could give you a few pointers about learning to jump him perhaps. Stay the night if you will."

"Wow, that would be great!" cried Owlie.

"Good-bye," said the doctor gravely, offering his hand, which enclosed the boy's in a firm grip.

He turned away and strode out the door, followed by Thomas Jennings, who glanced back at his son. "Take a look to see that your mother's sleeping, that she doesn't want anything," he said.

Owlie stood alone in the kitchen, gazing thoughtfully at the empty frying pan without seeing it. A strange realization had come to him. It hadn't mattered—it hadn't mattered a bit how the doctor looked, although his face was still horrifying to anyone who just thought of it as a face. The awful red welts, the down-twisted mouth, the misshapen jaw were still the same as the night when the sight had made him faint with fear. But inside that face was a human being who had come to the help of someone who was suffering. -

If the doctor were to walk to the village, Owlie knew it would be a miserable experience for him. People would turn away, sick at the sight. Little children would point and say, "What's the matter with that man?" How cruel, how stupid people could be! To think that he himself had taken pleasure in deciding that the mysterious stranger on the island was a loony who climbed trees to throw rocks at people!

When he had fainted with fear at the sight of a frightening face it must have been pretty hard on the doctor. Then another thought occurred to him. Perhaps when the gang yelled at him about his limp and his glasses and his shortness, they weren't thinking about how he felt, they were just being stupid.

With a serious look on his face he had turned to go upstairs to check on whether his mother wanted anything, when a heavy knock on the front door made him start with surprise.

Sam gave his rumbling bark and preceded the

boy into the hall, where he stood alternately barking and wagging his tail so that Owlie guessed he would not be opening the door to complete strangers.

To his astonishment he found himself face to face with Mr. Hammond and Mr. Dover.

"Look here, young fellow," said Mr. Hammond gruffly, "we want to have a word with you. Is your father home?"

"No," said Owlie. "But he'll be back soon," he added quickly. There was something in the expression of Mr. Hammond's eyes that made him uneasy.

Mr. Dover interrupted as Mr. Hammond opened his mouth to speak again. His heavy black eyebrows met over his thick nose in a scowl as he said, "I'm the witness; I saw you with that stone in your hand."

"You threw a stone at my horse," declared Mr. Hammond. "There was a big stone and a big stick lying in there where I keep the horses. He saw you." Mr. Hammond jerked his scrawny neck in Mr. Dover's direction. "He saw you with a stone in your hand. There wasn't anyone else around. You did it."

"No, I didn't!" exclaimed Owlie.

"Listen to him deny it," cried Mr. Dover. "Can

132

you stand there and tell me you didn't have a stone in your hand?"

Owlie remained silent.

"You threw a stone at my horse and made him jump out over the fence. When you found he was lame, you came sneaking back and took him away from me for practically nothing. I saw you riding him up in the village. He's a valuable horse." Mr. Hammond's face had turned very red. "I want him back."

The boy looked up at the two men, who glared down at him. He squared his shoulders. "I bought Mystery. He's mine," he said.

"Fraud and false pretenses!" exclaimed Mr. Hammond, his face becoming a shade redder. "Now don't make any trouble. Here's the forty dollars you paid for him. I want him back. I've got a witness to prove what I say is true." He nodded toward Mr. Dover.

"I'll talk to my father," said Owlie. He had turned very pale, and he held one hand inside the other behind his back so that the man couldn't thrust the money at him.

"Let's just take the horse and leave the forty dollars in the stable," said Mr. Hammond, moving away and pocketing his bills again.

"You can't do that; my father won't let you do that. He'll get the police." Owlie was trembling with emotion.

"Go easy; talk to his father," cautioned Mr. Dover, laying a hand on Mr. Hammond's arm. "We can take a look at the horse anyway. Maybe his father will be back soon, and we can make him see reason."

"If you take my horse I'll—I'll kill you!" cried Owlie, beside himself with rage and fear. But the men turned their backs and walked away.

With his mother lying helpless upstairs he felt he could not leave the house. He was forced to stand in the doorway, watching as the two men headed for the stable. He saw them open the door and disappear inside.

At the tone of fear in Owlie's voice Sam had begun to growl, and he stood now behind the screen door, his eyes fixed on the stable.

A wild plan was taking shape in Owlie's mind. First he would go upstairs as his father had directed and look to see if his mother was sleeping or whether she needed anything. Then he would come downstairs again, and if the men were leading Mystery from his stall, he would set Sam on them, grab Mystery, and gallop away to the island.

With cautious steps he tiptoed to the door of his parents' bedroom and peeked inside. On the big double bed his mother lay sleeping peacefully, so he stole away back down the stairs to rejoin Sam by the door.

"You'll get them if they try to take Mystery, won't you!" The boy laid a trembling hand on the dog's head. The realization had come to him that he couldn't possibly gallop away on his horse. He couldn't leave his mother even though his father would be returning soon.

If only he would come! Before very long he should be back; that is, unless the doctor had asked him to go ashore for some reason.

As he watched, the stable door opened and the two men came out. Walking side by side they headed for the dock. Owlie hurried to the kitchen window and saw that his father was about to land with the dory. He watched him deliberately ship his oars, make fast the painter to a ring, and climb slowly out of his boat to face the two men waiting for him.

They talked for some time, but at last the boy saw Mr. Hammond and Mr. Dover leave. His father turned toward the house. His face was grave as he came inside and met his son, who had hastened to the door to meet him.

"What's this all about?" he asked. "I want to hear your side of this story. Is your mother all right?"

"She's sleeping," said Owlie.

They went back into the kitchen and sat down at the table.

"Now tell me all about it," said Thomas Jennings.

"It was Bud who threw the stick and the stone. He beat it when he saw his father coming."

"But you had a stone too."

"Yes, I did."

"What were you going to do with it?"

"I picked it up for a paperweight for Mom. It's upstairs."

"You didn't give it to her?"

"No. It didn't seem nice anymore."

His father nodded as though he understood. "Why didn't you tell old Hammond that Bud did it?"

Owlie dropped his eyes. "Bud said he'd get me if I told."

Again his father nodded as though he understood.

"They say they'll take it to court. Hammond says he'll get a lawyer. He has Dover as a witness. He realizes he sold a valuable horse, and he intends to try to prove that you deliberately injured the horse so as to get him cheap."

"They can't take Mystery away from me, can they?" cried Owlie.

"I don't quite know. It would be your word against Bud's father's. We'll do everything possible. I don't know what the law says about a situation like this. Hammond says he'll give us until September to decide whether we want to settle quietly by giving up the horse. Otherwise he says he'll take it to court. I told them if they touched Mystery in the meantime, I'd make it hot for them."

"Three weeks and then we have to decide," said Owlie, nervously pushing his glasses up on his nose.

"Look here, son, let's find out what Dr. Delafield thinks about it. He asked you to ride over to the island. I'll deliver your papers with the car Sunday morning. You could go Saturday afternoon and spend the night."

"That's a good idea," said Owlie. "If they ever came and got Mystery, I'd—I'd—"

"I don't think they'd dare," said his father.

TWELVE

It was the late afternoon of a calm bright day when Owlie, mounted on Mystery and followed by Sam, splashed ashore at Hideaway Island.

The doctor stepped forward to greet them. "If I didn't know the secret of the sand bar, I would have thought you were walking on the water!" he said.

"It's a lot easier than last time; the tide's nice and low," said Owlie. He kicked his feet out of the stirrups and patted Mystery's neck.

Sam shook himself and had a good roll in the fine white sand. When he stood up he looked as if he were powdered with sugar.

"I hope you've come for the night," said the doctor, laying a hand on the horse's damp shoulder.

"Yes, I brought Mystery's grain." Owlie unslung from his back the canvas bag he used when delivering newspapers. He eased it to the ground and vaulted off, then pulled the reins over his horse's head.

"Why don't you unsaddle and turn him loose?" suggested the doctor.

"Okay," agreed Owlie.

Stripping off Mystery's saddle and bridle, the boy laid them on a rock above the tide line.

The horse, feeling free, gave a long shuddering shake, and sinking to his knees, lay down in the sand and rolled completely over. When he got up he shook himself again, then wandered off into the trees. Soon they saw him up the path, drinking out of the spring and cropping some grass that grew nearby.

"How about gathering firewood, Owlie. We might have a campfire on the beach and cook our supper. I have two sleeping bags. Would you like to sleep outdoors tonight? Then tomorrow morning we could start a little jumping."

"Sure," said Owlie. "That would be great."

"While you're getting the wood, I'll get the food up at the shack," said the doctor as he started along the path among the rocks.

Owlie pulled off his shoes and socks and rolled up the legs of his blue jeans. The sand felt warm and good between his toes. Followed by Sam, he strolled along the shore, stopping from time to time to pick up a piece of driftwood or a broken pine branch. The rocks were hot, so he cooled the soles of his feet by stepping into the water.

He returned to the strip of beach with a good armful of wood. There he dropped his load but afterward went back twice along the shore to drag up larger pieces he had noticed earlier.

Crossing small twigs and pieces of dried bark, he was laying the fire when the doctor arrived with a frying pan and other supplies.

"That looks all right," Dr. Delafield said briskly. "Here's a match."

Soon a thin trail of blue smoke rose in the still air, and a few crackles and pops showed that the fire had really caught. Owlie carefully laid on some larger twigs and then some good-sized sticks and finally a branch or two.

The doctor had arranged strips of bacon in a frying pan and opened a can of beans, which he set on a rock above the sand.

"We might pick a few blueberries, and then we could have blueberry pancakes for dessert," he suggested, handing Owlie a tin cup. "Will Sam eat the bacon?" he asked.

"He won't if I tell him not to," replied Owlie.

"Look, Sam!" cried the boy, grabbing the big dog's collar and turning his head toward the rock where the pan rested. "Don't touch!" he commanded in a firm voice.

Sam wagged his tail and turned his head away.

"We'll find some blueberries off here," said the doctor, leading the way over the rocks into the pines.

Presently they came upon a cleared area, where a couple of jumps made out of poles were set up. "Here's where we'll practice tomorrow," said the doctor. "I thought you'd come, so I got these ready."

They walked on a little farther. Under their feet mealy plumb vine, whose glossy green leaves grew thick and matted, made a springy carpet. The warm air was full of the spicy fragrance of pine needles and sweet fern, and suddenly he saw the patch of blueberry bushes just ahead. The first berries Owlie picked rattled into his tin cup, and then as it became fuller, they dropped with soft plops on the blue heap in the bottom.

Before very long the boy and the man each had half a cupful, and they made their way back to the fire, which had burned down to glowing embers.

"Just right to cook bacon," said the doctor briskly,

and he brought the frying pan and held it over the heat. Soon the smell of wood smoke and frying bacon made Owlie so hungry he asked, "What can I do to help?"

"Get me one of those tin plates," said the doctor. "I have a special way of fixing up the beans. There's a package of rolls you can split open too."

With a long fork he lifted the bacon, which was beginning to crisp, onto the plate. He poured some bacon fat over the rolls which he set by the fire to warm, then scraped the baked beans from the can into the frying pan. Over the beans he poured a good dollop of molasses, stirred in a little mustard, and put the bacon on top.

"This is baked beans Delafield," said the doctor with satisfaction. "Wait till you taste them." He set the pan near the fire to keep warm and began stirring the pancake batter, making it from a prepared mix and canned milk. "Get me a cup of water from the spring to dilute this milk," he instructed Owlie.

"We'll dump in the blueberries and let this stand while we eat our first course," said the doctor to Owlie, who had returned with the cup of fresh water.

Sam sat near the fire, sneezing from time to time when smoke blew in his face and drooling in anticipation of supper.

"Hey, Sam, I'll get your dog biscuits," said Owlie. He turned toward the feed bag he had dropped on the ground, but the doctor stopped him with a gesture.

"Open up a couple of tins of beef for your dog," he directed. "I don't believe baked beans would be much to his taste, and dog biscuits sound a little dry and unappetizing, somewhat like eating crackers while you watch everyone else enjoying a three-course meal with gravy. Here's an extra plate. Scoop the beef onto this. Here, Sam, come on. Are you hungry?" he asked the dog, who came toward them, sniffing at the sound of his name and the smell of meat in the freshly opened cans.

"We always give him one meal of meat at home," said Owlie, "but I thought dog biscuits would be easier to carry in my bag. He had some meat this morning."

"He's a big dog with a big appetite; I can see that," said Dr. Delafield, smiling.

Owlie threw another branch on the fire to keep it going, then took the plate of beans the doctor dished up for him and laid a hot roll on the edge. He seated himself on a rock and looked out over the water, glinting in the low rays of the sun.

The first forkful of hot mealy beans melted in his mouth and soon his plate was empty.

"Have some more," urged the doctor.

"Aren't you going to have some?" asked Owlie.

"No, I think I'll wait for the pancakes, but you're a growing boy. Have some more. Finish them up." The doctor, pan in hand, towered over Owlie sitting on his rock and dished beans onto his plate.

The boy looked up at him. "Does eating a lot make you grow?" he asked.

"Well, yes," said Dr. Delafield, glancing quickly at Owlie. "To a certain extent it does. Inherited bone structure from some ancestor has a lot to do with it too."

With smacking licks of his tongue Sam cleaned a few clinging meat scraps from the black fur of his jaws. Then he sniffed at his dish and lapped around the corners to be sure he hadn't missed anything.

"Hey, Mystery, where are you?" shouted Owlie. He got up from the rock and picked up the bag of grain. "Come on, feed time," he called.

The thudding of a trot could be heard and the horse appeared, head held high, ears pricked. He stopped beside the boy and gave a low whinny while he gently bumped Owlie with his head.

"I always call 'feed time' when I'm going to feed him grain," explained Owlie, who began shaking out a good measure of oats onto a flat rock.

"Yes, horses can get to understand a few words that are repeated often under the same circumstances," agreed the doctor. He watched the animal lower his head to the yellow oats. "Tell me," he asked, "how did you train him to stand so quietly for mounting? I remember that night when your mother was hurt, and you came to get me. You could feel the horse was excited and eager to be off, but he stood like a rock while we both mounted. It was really unusual, really extraordinary."

"The girl who raised him trained him to stand like that while she stood up on his back and picked apples. Then she always bit off a piece and gave it to him. I usually give him something after I've mounted too. Dr. Little, the vet, said he was started right when he was young. That's why he has such good manners."

"She stood on his back to pick apples," repeated the doctor. "Well, that reminds me of something. But never mind now, let's get these pancakes cooking. Wash out the frying pan, will you? Take some sand and scour it."

Owlie carried the pan to the water's edge, and with handfuls of wet sand he cleaned out the last of the beans, rinsed it, and brought it back clean and shining to the doctor.

"Good!" he exclaimed. "Now I'll grease it with a little oil. Salty fat like bacon grease or butter makes things stick. This is better." With a bit of paper, he wiped over the surface and removed all the surplus oil, then held the pan over the fire to heat it.

"Pour in about a quarter of a cup of the batter, Owlie, and hand me that flat thing for turning," ordered the doctor. "Oh, yes, and unscrew the cap of the maple syrup, put the butter on a plate, and hand me another plate."

At each of the doctor's directions, Owlie jumped to obey. As he strove to execute Dr. Delafield's commands promptly, he wondered whether interns in the operating room felt the same way.

"What do you want to be when you grow up?" asked the doctor suddenly.

Was this mental telepathy? Owlie wondered. "I want to be a doctor," he said.

"Good," replied Dr. Delafield.

"But I don't know whether I'll be able to make it," added the boy. "College and medical school cost a lot. I hope so though. I'm going to try."

"Where there's a will there's a way," said the doctor briefly as he flipped the golden brown pancake onto its other side. There were little round bumps where the blueberries showed in the batter. Owlie's mouth began to water.

"Eat this while it's hot," ordered the doctor.

Golden butter melted on top of the pancake and an amber flood of syrup dripped over the edges onto the tin plate, which Dr. Delafield handed to him. In all, Owlie accounted for five.

When they had eaten they scoured the forks and dishes with sand and laid everything together beside a rock.

Sitting by the fire, they looked out across the water, which was turning pink in the sunset. The tide was rising and lapping higher on Turtle Rock. Gray and white gulls planed lazily in the still air, giving occasional cries. From far out at sea, beyond the mouth of the harbor, came the slow tolling of a bell buoy, rocking gently on the swells. A homeward-bound sailboat, making slow progress in the light breeze, was headed for her mooring. The sails dropped slowly like tired wings and were furled. Then the crew rowed ashore in a skiff and landed far up the beach at a house where lamplight glowed.

Night was beginning to settle over the harbor. On the point the lighthouse began its slow wink.

The silence was broken by the doctor's voice.

"Safe harbor," he said. "That's what my wife and I called the shack on this island. In Chicago I was always busy; life was hectic. When we came to Westerly in the summer, I craved quiet and the sound of gulls and the lap of water on the rocks. We enjoyed having guests at the house, but on Hideaway Island we made a point of never inviting anyone. It was our rule. You, Owlie, are the first person to be invited."

"Oh," said Owlie. He felt overwhelmed by receiving an older person's confidence but at the same time pleased.

"I love the sea. It's been my dream someday to retire and live at Westerly." The doctor rose and dragged another branch onto the fire, which flared up and highlighted the horror of his scarred and twisted face. He sat down again and leaned back against a rock. "But I'm not an old man yet," he said. "I want to work. I'm trying to decide what I'll do instead of practicing medicine. Most of my patients have been children. I couldn't walk through the wards of a hospital looking the way I do. I'd scare the wits out of them."

His attempt at a laugh cut into Owlie's heart. "Well, you don't scare me," he said.

"You're used to me now," said the doctor dryly.

"Other people could be too," said the boy.

The man grunted in disbelief and changed the subject. "How did you come to be called Owlie?" he asked.

"My glasses," replied the boy.

"Hmm," said the doctor. "Would you rather people called you something else?"

"No, it's my name now."

"Yes, one gets used to a nickname," said the doctor. "I remember a boy named Samuel, who was in my class at school. He was very popular. Captain of the football team, as a matter of fact. His nickname was Slimy Sewer Pipe."

Owlie laughed.

"Nicknames are all right," said the doctor. "A rose by any other name would have just as long thorns."

"Smell as sweet," corrected Owlie.

The doctor smiled his twisted smile. "You know, those glasses you're wearing don't fit. Glasses can be very becoming to people. In fact when you are used to a person wearing glasses, you don't like to see him without."

The boy had taken his off and was swinging them around in his hand. "I can see better at a distance without them," he said.

"You have the eyes of a sailor," said the doctor. "What sports do you enjoy at school?"

Owlie was silent. "Oh, nothing much," he said finally.

"Because you're a little lame," said the doctor quickly.

"Um," said Owlie. If it hadn't been dark, it would have been harder to listen to the doctor's gentle but insistent questions.

"Sometimes handicaps spur people on to greater efforts in the fields where they *can* succeed. In fact handicaps have made people great. It's what is inside people that counts. Not the outside." He paused, then continued with assumed lightness. "Maybe now that I've got a face that would scare patients into a relapse, I'll be forced to become a sculptor or a steeplejack or something." There was a quizzical expression in his eyes as he looked at Owlie.

"Do you think I'll grow some more?" asked the boy in a choked voice. He surprised himself by saying it out loud.

"Of course you will," said the doctor with conviction. "You won't be a very tall man probably, but what does it really matter? A doctor doesn't have to pick up his patients and carry them around. You'd probably not succeed as a stevedore on the docks, handling two-hundred-pound crates, but that's not what you were cut out to do. You have brains, Owlie. Use them. Contribute to the welfare of the human race, and you will find your own happiness along the way."

They were quiet for a few moments, watching the fire where the logs were turning a hot red-gold. Suddenly Owlie spoke.

"Do you think Mystery's going to be all right loose on the island all night?" he asked.

"Certainly," said the doctor. "He loves it."

"I wonder if he'll step on us while we're asleep?" asked the boy.

"No, horses never step on people if they can help it. Haven't you ever seen pictures of people who have fallen in a race? Horses jump over them or go around them; they never step on them."

"Sam steps all over me," said Owlie.

"Well, a horse won't," said the doctor.

At the sound of his name, the dog rose from where he had been lying on the sand, and pushing his black face toward his master, lifted an affectionate paw, which he placed on the boy's leg.

"Let's take the picnic things back to the shack and pick up our sleeping bags," said the doctor.

It had been a good idea to collect everything together while it was still light. They divided the

151

load between them, and with the man leading the way on the familiar path, they set off through the darkness.

Inside the shack shadows leaped on the wall as the oil lamp was lit, and the boy remembered the night when a reassuring voice had spoken to quiet his fear as he lay on that bed in the corner. It seemed funny now to remember his feeling of terror. He began to examine the maps and pictures of sailing ships tacked to the walls.

The doctor was busying himself opening a big sea chest with brass handles. "Here's your sleeping bag," he said. "Let's go back to the fire and turn in for the night."

Beside the path in the darkness they heard the snuffling of a horse, and Owlie gave Mystery's shadowy neck a pat or two before he followed Dr. Delafield, who had gone to the fire and kicked the logs together. A waving banner of flame threw fiery snakes into the darkness, where they disintegrated into sparks which were snuffed out in the high cool air under the stars.

A moment later, from his sleeping bag, the doctor called, "Good night, sleep well."

Owlie snuggled down deep in his own bag, which smelled pleasantly of moth balls. He felt Sam flop down next to him and then the weight of the dog's head on his legs. Together they listened to the soft continuous murmur of ripples coming up on the smooth sand of the shore.

As the boy dropped off to sleep he thought drowsily, I never asked the doctor about Mr. Hammond wanting Mystery. Somehow, on Hideaway Island, everything seemed so safe that worries were left behind on the mainland.

THIRTEEN

The rising sun woke Owlie, who rolled away from Sam and peered out of his sleeping bag. A strong breeze was chopping the harbor water and giving a bumpy ride to gray and white gulls. All at once, with mewing cries, the birds rose into the air. Slowly fanning their curved wings, they planed sideways on a current of air and swooped low toward where he was lying, so that he noticed their staring yellow eyes hungrily searching.

They see something left from the picnic, and they're trying to get up nerve to grab it, speculated Owlie.

With a wriggle he extricated himself from his sleeping bag while observing that the doctor must have risen before the sun, for there was no sign of him.

Beside the burned-out campfire lay two rolls that had fallen into the sand the night before. He picked them up and threw them far out onto the water, whereat the gulls' cries redoubled into a quarrelsome tumult as they dove to retrieve their prize.

The idea of some breakfast for himself was most appealing, but he decided to have a swim before going to look for Dr. Delafield. Stripping off his clothes, he waded into the water, which gave him a cold shock so early in the morning. But he dove under to avoid being splashed by Sam, who was following closely behind.

When he turned to head toward shore, he saw Mystery trotting out of the pines. The horse's black mane crested on his neck as with head held high and tail raised he trotted lightly in the direction of the spot where he had found oats the night before.

"Just a second, I'll open the bag," called Owlie. The horse whinnied when he saw the boy; then circled impatiently, lowering his head and snuffling at the bag lying on the ground.

Owlie poured the last of the oats onto the flat rock on which he had put the feed the night before, and Mystery shoved his nose eagerly into the sliding pile of grain.

The wind was cool and the boy shivered. Hastily

he pulled his clothes onto his damp body. "It's all right for you and Sam without shirts—you've got fur," said Owlie, looking at his horse.

Shaking sand out of his shoes, he sat down to put them on while he watched a sloop sailing up harbor. All her canvas was set and brilliant white in the rising sun. Her bow slapped the water and drove spray over the deck as she spanked along in the choppy sea, heeling to port in the stiff breeze from the west.

The boy kept his eyes on her and thought he would like to be aboard, his hand on the tiller. Again the question came to his mind, How had the doctor arrived on the island? A boat of any size was unable to land because of the shoals and rocks. It was treacherous sailing anywhere near Hideaway Island, yet the doctor had managed to come here. How had he done it? Well, he'd ask him, Owlie decided.

"Hey, Sam, come on," he called, and leaving Mystery to finish his grain, he walked up the path toward the shack.

In a little kitchen, no larger than a ship's galley, which opened off the main room, Dr. Delafield was scrambling eggs. The lingering scent of last night's oil lamp mingled with the morning smell of coffee and toast and the woody smell of unfinished bare-board walls.

"Hello," said the doctor. "Sleep well?"

"Sure," said Owlie. "So did Sam. How did you get here from Chicago?" he asked abruptly.

"Come on and eat and I'll tell you." Dr. Delafield carried two plates of eggs and toast to the table.

"Would you rather have cocoa than coffee?" he asked. "I made some."

"Yes, thanks," said Owlie.

They pulled two straight-backed chairs to the table and sat down. The eggs were nice and creamy —not overcooked—and the toast was hot and spread with butter and marmalade.

"The way I got here was very simple," said Dr. Delafield. "A young doctor I know drove me from Chicago. I feel a bit self-conscious about having people look at my face at the moment, as you know, so we traveled mostly by night to my brother's house on the coast near Boston. He sailed me over here the next day. His sloop draws a lot of water, so he anchored off the island, and I put my things in the skiff he had been towing and rowed ashore. I have a short-wave radio in the kitchen. He keeps in touch with me, and if I want him to, he'll come back to pick me up."

"Where's the skiff?" asked Owlie.

"Pulled up behind some bayberry bushes. I seldom use it."

"Only when you go to Westerly to get books in the night," said Owlie.

"That's right," agreed the doctor. He gathered up the empty plates. "All set for a jumping lesson?" he asked.

"Sure," Owlie replied.

"You go and saddle up, and I'll wash these dishes. I'll meet you in the clearing in the woods where I've set up jumps. Will you be able to catch your horse easily?"

"I think so," said Owlie, "but I might just take along some sugar or an apple or something."

"Here's a carrot," said the doctor.

"Thank you," said Owlie. "Sam must have stayed with Mystery, I guess. I called him, but he didn't come. I'll get those dog biscuits out of the bag and give them to him. He's had his exercise, so he'll be about ready for breakfast."

"Shorten your stirrups up a hole; they looked too long yesterday when you rode toward me," called the doctor as the boy went out the door and started down the path.

Mystery came when Owlie called and accepted the carrot. Shortly afterward Sam returned from a morning stroll and ate the dog biscuits with sharp crunches of his strong teeth, then sat down, ears twitching, and waited to see what was going to happen next. He looked at his master expectantly.

By hanging onto the horse's mane with his right hand and his nose with his left, the boy led Mystery to the rock where the saddle and bridle had been placed.

After he tacked up, he obeyed the doctor's instructions and raised each stirrup one hole. He felt the girth to be sure it was tight enough, checked the throat latch on the bridle to be sure it was fastened just right, then mounted, and followed by Sam, rode off into the woods.

He was feeling a little nervous at the idea of jumping. He remembered the hard fall on his back which had knocked out his wind the time Mystery jumped the big drainage pipe.

Riding along the edge of the pines, keeping near the shoreline, the boy could hear the lap and chuckle of waves slapping at the rocks. All about him was the spicy scent of sweet fern and bayberry leaves crushed under his horse's hoofs.

He found the doctor in the clearing setting up

a series of low poles, spaced about five feet apart and raised slightly off the ground.

"Lucky I hadn't cut up these poles for firewood," he said. "They aren't really thick enough, but they'll do. The theory of these poles is to collect your horse and slow him down before he jumps. He has to go over all these in rhythmic strides and then take the jump at the end."

The doctor laid a hand on one of Owlie's knees and pressed it into the saddle. "Lean forward and stand slightly up in your stirrups. That's your jumping position. Push your hands up on the horse's neck and give him a free head. Keep forward all the time so you don't come back on his mouth. Snatching a horse hurts him and discourages his jumping.

"Just go quietly at a trot the first time or two. Keep your position. Go ahead. That's right; keep him squarely at it. Press with your legs."

The boy felt the horse under him, springy and eager. He kept a steady contact by means of the reins on the light snaffle in Mystery's mouth and trotted him slowly toward the poles.

The horse had never been frightened or excited while jumping, so he went calmly and obediently.

The series of poles, raised about a foot off the

ground, slowed the horse's pace as he stepped delicately over them at a steady trot. When the little jump appeared in front of him at the end, he popped it quietly and easily as Owlie pushed his hands forward to give his horse a free head.

"Good!" cried the doctor. "That was very good."

The lesson lasted an hour. Toward the end the doctor had spaced the poles farther apart and they cantered over them and cleared a much bigger jump in fine form. Owlie's face was alight with happiness. But suddenly it sobered. Now was the time to get advice about Mr. Hammond's unreasonable demand. He walked his horse over to where the doctor stood.

"Do you know that man who keeps a livery stable near your place?" he asked.

"Hammond, you mean?"

"Yes. He sold me Mystery for forty dollars because he was lame, now he wants to buy him back."

"You don't want to sell him, I'm sure."

"No. But he says I have to. Mr. Dover saw me standing by the barn with a stone in my hand when Mystery jumped over the fence and hurt himself. He says he's a witness that I threw stones to make him jump out."

"Did you?"

"No, I didn't." Owlie's voice had become very tense.

"What made him jump out then?"

"Bud Dover. He threw things at the horses. He saw his father coming and beat it. So I was the only one left."

"What were you doing with a stone?" the doctor asked sternly.

"I was going to give it to my mother for a paperweight." He wanted to say it was pretty but something stopped him. He felt silly even telling as much as he had.

The doctor nodded, and Owlie saw that he was believed.

"Why don't you go to Bud and tell him to explain to his father that it wasn't you?"

"Because"—Owlie hesitated—"because he said he'd get me."

"When could he do that?"

"On the way from the bus. I have to walk home from the bus stop with him nearly every day."

"Has he ever done anything to you before?"

"Yes," said Owlie. Then he broke out savagely. "I wish I could punch him, but he's too big."

"How does Hammond think he's going to make you sell the horse back?"

"He says if I don't do it by the first of September he'll go to court, and Mr. Dover will be his witness. I haven't any witness for me."

"Owlie, if Hammond goes through with this, I'll help you. I don't know just how, but I'll help you."

"Thanks," said Owlie feelingly. He leaned forward in the saddle and patted Mystery's neck. It was nice of the doctor to want to be helpful, but what could he possibly do? He hadn't been there to see that it was really Bud who threw the stone.

FOURTEEN

At four o'clock one morning, just before dawn, Owlie awoke to the sound of rain being flung against his window like handfuls of pebbles. It was still dark and a nor'easter was blowing strongly in off the sea. He lay listening to the wind and felt the house tremble while every window rattled and every door shook.

He had just had a dream that left him very shaken. In the dream he saw Mystery all skin and bones and covered with burrs. Mr. Hammond was riding on his back. The horse's eyes looked pleadingly at Owlie, but just then the man raised a long whip and struck the horse between the ears.

"Stop!" cried Owlie in the dream. But Mr. Hammond sat there laughing, and as Owlie sprang forward to wrest the whip from his hand, he woke up.

It was hard to go back to sleep. A sickening remembrance of Mystery looking hungry and unhappy stayed in his mind, making the dream seem like reality.

At last the faint gray light of a troubled dawn showed through his window while he listened to the storm, which went on unabated. The tumult made him think of an orchestral piece. The moaning wind rising to a high pitch was like a choir of voices accompanied by the kettledrums of the rattling shutters and the bass drums of the thumping doors. In a pause of the storm he heard a song sparrow whose notes sounded like a flute, hopeful and gay. Then the percussion instruments of doors, windows, and shutters took over again and accompanied the shrieking wind.

It was going to be awful delivering papers. He wondered whether he could do it. Bed was cozy; bed was good. He pulled the sheet over his head to shut out the beginning of daylight and fell into a deep sleep.

The sound of his parents walking downstairs and Sam shaking himself outside his door awakened him, and he lay there half remembering the nightmare he had had earlier.

Indeed, even while he dressed he could not quite rid his mind of the haunting feeling that something was wrong with his horse. He needed to put his hand on Mystery's sleek sides and hear the low nicker he always gave when Owlie went into his stall each morning.

Preparations for breakfast were going on in the kitchen as he put on his oilskins and rubber boots to keep him dry on his walk to the stable.

When he opened the front door, wind blew rain into his face, and he closed it behind him quickly.

The path was soaking wet. He walked head down but when he raised his eyes he was startled to see a figure in a rain coat standing by the white picket gate. Under a too large sou'wester hat that dripped with rain, the face was indistinguishable. But as Owlie approached he saw that it was Bud Dover, although he couldn't hear what Bud was saying, for the high wind carried his voice away.

Bud beckoned him nearer and Owlie reluctantly complied.

"I want to tell you something," said Bud. His voice was surly and threatening. Owlie noticed that his broken tooth was beginning to turn black.

"What's the matter?" asked Owlie.

"Do you know what day today is?" asked Bud.

"Monday, August twenty-fifth," said Owlie. "What of it?"

"Pretty near the first of September. Are you going to give back that horse?"

"No," said Owlie. He had turned very pale. He

pushed his rain-spattered glasses up on his nose and lifted his head to look at Bud's face, which was bent toward him in an ugly fashion.

"Well, you'd better give him back. Mr. Hammond means it. He's going to take it to court if you don't."

"Let him," said Owlie stoutly. In his imagination he felt the doctor's presence at his elbow, and his voice carried conviction.

Bud looked visibly shaken and glared at Owlie. "Remember what I said I'd do if you told."

"You wouldn't dare."

"Yes, I would. If my father ever found out, he'd be so mad he wouldn't get me a car when I'm sixteen. He'd be really sore. He told me if I didn't get in any bad trouble he'd buy me a secondhand car when I can get a license. It would be your fault if I didn't get it."

The logic of this was hard for Owlie to understand, but he saw that Bud was deadly serious.

"I'm going to tell your father and Mr. Hammond it was you," said Owlie. "My father will tell them too."

"If you dare!" cried Bud, doubling up his fist. "You haven't a witness!" he declared, suddenly triumphant.

"I don't care. I won't give up my horse," said Owlie, and he turned his back and walked off toward the stable.

With a shaking hand he picked up the hay fork and pitched Mystery's breakfast into a corner of the stall. The horse whinnied softly and lowered his head to the feed. Owlie laid a hand on his smooth bay neck, then pushed back into place a strand of black mane which had strayed to the wrong side.

"They can't take you from me," he muttered passionately, and laying his forehead against the horse's warm flank, he remained a few moments quite motionless while a tear forced itself out of his left eye and traveled down his nose.

With a sniff he straightened up, took off his glasses and wiped them. Mystery cocked an ear back to listen to Owlie's voice and went calmly on eating hay. The boy patted the horse's rump as he left. Outside the stall, he closed the sliding bolt on the door and went back to the house, pushing against the strong wind as if it were a solid thing.

His mother, her arm still held in a sling, greeted him with a smile. "Fried cornmeal mush and syrup," she spelled with her fingers, knowing it was his favorite breakfast. His father was just finishing and rose from the table as Owlie seated himself. "I must go up to Westerly and check that everything's made fast—this wind is almost gale force," he said.

In spite of the fact that Owlie wanted to detain his father and tell him about the encounter with Bud, the boy knew that his problem could wait; while up at Westerly a shutter might have come loose in the storm or some shingles on the roof might have blown up, letting in the rain. So he said nothing. Nor did he at the moment confide in his mother. Both Owlie and his father tended to protect her from unpleasant news as long as possible. They hated to see her smiling face cloud over. Right now she looked so happy standing at the stove and dishing up something she knew he liked. When the plate of crisp, golden-brown fried mush was set down before him, Owlie's mouth began to water. He poured on syrup generously from the jug and thought vaguely as the first delicious spoonful melted on his tongue that there was a lot of comfort for worries in the good taste of food.

Hopping from perch to perch in its brass-barred cage, the canary finally decided on the perfect spot to pause and deliver one of those piercing serenades that canaries enjoy. The harsh notes offended Owlie's ears, which he felt like plugging up with his fingers. But his mother didn't even turn around. Strange to think that she couldn't hear a single sound. What would it be like to be deaf, he wondered? Worse to be blind. He closed his eyes a moment and then opened them, feeling lucky.

Rising, he touched his mother gently on the shoulder to attract her attention and spelled out, "Going to deliver the papers."

"In this storm?" she spelled back, looking amazed.

Owlie nodded confidently and moved his fingers rapidly to say, "Keep my glasses; they'll get all wet." He and Mystery would make it, he knew. The only problem was to keep the papers dry. But in the past people had been pretty good about watching for him on a rainy day and coming out to their porches to take the paper from his hand.

The thought of a ride in the storm exhilarated him. There was no real danger except from falling trees branches or flying objects picked up by the gale. He led his horse out and mounted.

As they trotted along the muddy road Mystery's neck was arched and his ears were pricked up, looking for any occasion to shy as a protest against the weather. Rain blew into their faces, and Owlie bent his head and half closed his eyes against the storm. Rivulets of water ran off his hat and down his oilskins, while Mystery's coat was dark and wet. Where deep puddles had formed on the road, falling drops of rain made it look as though the puddles were full of jumping minnows. By the time they completed half the route, the rain had let up somewhat. However, the wind continued unabated and slashed at the leaves of trees that bent before its force. Small branches had been torn off and lay in the wet road and in front of Dr. Smith's house a large limb had fallen.

As he had foreseen, his customers were waiting for him. The girl who had given Mystery sugar was out in a storm coat and seemed to be enjoying the buffeting of the gale. Her hair was blown across her eyes and she was laughing as she hung onto a post for support.

But at the next house something happened that upset Owlie greatly. The grumpy man who had told him not to let it happen again when he had once been late with the papers was waiting just inside the door and popped out looking like a surly gnome, his coat collar turned up to his red ears. "I'm hearing some rumors about how you acquired that fine horse of yours," he said, scowling at Owlie. "I'm thinking that perhaps I'd rather not do business with a boy like you."

Owlie was too dumbfounded to reply. He handed over the man's paper and continued on, sick at heart. All of a sudden the joyous pride he had always felt in his beautiful horse turned into an uneasy feeling that people watching him go by were saying, "Have you heard how he managed to get that horse? He deliberately lamed him so he could buy him for forty dollars!"

The injustice of the man's remark rankled in his mind. He couldn't shake it off. How many people felt the same way? he wondered. He realized Mr. Hammond and Mr. Dover must have been talking around the village. It made him feel like going home and hiding away from people. Anger and resentment welled up in his heart. In his frustration he sought some way to let off steam.

They passed again the village doctor's white clapboard house. The fallen limb of the elm tree had narrowly missed striking a for-sale sign that hung out in front. When Dr. Smith's father died, the doctor had moved to a distant city where he had inherited a large piece of property. Owlie knew that everyone in the village was complaining because there was no doctor. It was a nuisance to have to go all the way to Beachport to obtain prescriptions for their pills. The thought of the town made Owlie's mind drift in that direction, and suddenly he knew what he wanted to do.

Sam was sniffing at the picket fence, missing Dr. Smith's dog, who always used to growl at him. "Come on," cried Owlie, "let's look at the waves out beyond the point."

They cut down a short street onto a sand track that led to the water and set off in the direction of Beachport, following the shoreline of the harbor. Ahead lay the exposed drainage pipe, but no longer did a sense of apprehension grip him at the sight, for his first jumping lesson had been followed by many others that the doctor had given him on the island, and his confidence had grown.

At a brisk canter he headed straight for the obstacle, and Mystery sailed over it with a soaring leap, continuing his smooth stride after landing, while Owlie stayed well forward, sticking close to the saddle.

Now they could hear the roar of the breakers on the outer beach.

As they rounded the point the boy waved to the lighthouse keeper, who was struggling with a wind-blown canvas that had broken loose from a boat pulled up on the shore. Mystery pretended to be very frightened by the flapping sail and shied and then gave a buck. But Owlie only laughed and admonished him. "Steady, boy." Nothing his horse did now alarmed Owlie, who understood just how far he would go in misbehaving. It even made him feel happy when Mystery showed off, for it meant he felt well. It seemed a long time ago when a poor thin horse had limped down the lane from Mr. Hammond's barn.

Now he turned inland, away from the shore, for the storm-driven waves were rolling in and inundating the outer beach. The series of concrete breakwaters thrusting out into the water were like the spread fingers of a hand protecting the land from the destructive force of the pounding water. One minute he could see them and then a wave would cover one or more. Suddenly they looked to Owlie like a series of jumps and he vowed that on a calmer day he would go over them. The thought made his blood tingle, for they were solid and high.

On the land above the beach he walked his horse along, watching the majesty and power of the waves, crested with blown spray, as they broke on the shore with a pounding boom and then hissingly retreated, rolling big stones in the backwash.

Gradually the angry churning of his mind, boiling over what the surly little man had said, began to seem a small and insignificant disturbance compared to the furious might he was beholding. The anger went out of him and was swallowed up in the greater fury of the storm.

The blowing sand stung his face, and he began to worry about Mystery's eyes, for the horse was moving impatiently, signifying discomfort. Pressing with his legs and tightening the left rein, he turned and was about to start for home when he noticed a car that had drawn up on the Beachport road, which curved away about a hundred feet from where he was standing. Three occupants had alighted and were waving their arms to bid him approach. "Come on, Sam" said Owlie, "let's see what they want."

He trotted Mystery in the direction of the car, but as he got a little closer he was tempted for a moment to turn back, for he suddenly realized that it was Bud Dover and his father. Only because Roy Bladen was with them did he continue on. Roy's kind face appeared in sharp contrast to Bud's swaggering attitude and silly grin. What do they want? he wondered.

The wind was blowing their raincoats against their bodies, and Bud's hair, which needed cutting, was plastered over his eyes. Mystery approached with mincing steps, ears pricked, neck arched, ready to shy.

Owlie pulled up in front of them. He saw that

176

Bud had a freshly bandaged hand and decided they must have driven to Beachport to take him to the doctor.

"I just wanted to have a word with you," said Mr. Dover. He tried to lay a hand on Mystery's bridle, but the horse backed away from him sharply, jerking his head sideways at the man's sudden gesture. Sam took his place beside the horse as if facing the enemy.

"Look here," said the man, "I hope you and your father have decided to be sensible. Hammond means it, you know. He wants that horse back and he's going to get him."

"No, he's not," said Owlie tensely. He saw Roy looking at him. Unlike Bud and Mr. Dover, his face was calm and attentive. He seemed to be trying to read Owlie's expression, so as to know his thoughts. He is looking for the truth, thought Owlie, and suddenly he decided that no matter what the consequences might be, he would tell it.

"I didn't throw that stone; it was Bud," said Owlie.

"You dirty little liar!" cried Mr. Dover.

Bud's face contorted with rage. "Yes, liar!" he screamed. His face had turned very white, and it was hard to tell whether he was shaking or whether it was the wind blowing his raincoat.

"What do you mean by daring to say such a thing about my son?" shouted Mr. Dover. "Of all the cowardly, dirty tricks trying to put something off on my boy, when you know you did it yourself. I saw you with a stone, and no one else was there. You can't deny it!"

Bud was waving his fists belligerently and glaring at Owlie. It almost seemed as if he believed the story, having heard it told so many times.

Sam had begun to growl. The hair was rising along his back.

"Steady," said Mr. Dover, suddenly laying a restraining hand on Bud's arm. "We'll settle this in court in a few day's time. Don't wave your hand around like that—you'll start it bleeding. Then you won't be able to go to your girlfriend's party in Beachport tonight." He gave a forced laugh as he eyed Sam uneasily. "One more thing," he said as he turned away. "People have seen you swimming that horse of yours over to Dr. Delafield's island. That's going to be brought out against you in court, I'll tell you. No respect for law and order or private property. I know someone who's written the doctor in Chicago to tell him just what you're doing."

Roy Bladen stepped forward and laid a quiet hand on Mystery's neck. "Want to go swimming sometime, Owlie?" he asked. "I'll call you."

FIFTEEN

Roy's friendly gesture had eased the hurt in Owlie's heart. However, he was not certain whether by his action Roy had wanted to convey that he thought him innocent or whether his words were in response to an idea of good sportsmanship. Perhaps he didn't care to see two pitted against one.

When Owlie rose from his knees after saying his growing prayer and got into bed, a terrible ache of loneliness came over him. He felt as if everyone in the village—boys, girls, and grown-ups alike—probably believed Mr. Dover's story and were ranged against him. He imagined them all thinking, We don't want to do business with a boy like that. When he closed his eyes, he saw the surly face of the little man who had actually said the words out loud as he took his paper from Owlie's hand.

The boy's only comfort, and it was a big one, came from having talked to his father.

"If they sue we'll get a lawyer and fight," his father had said grimly.

It crossed Owlie's mind that Dr. Delafield too had said he would help. But how could he, way off on the island and unwilling to come ashore and meet people? It was nice of him to want to though.

In the darkness of his room he curled himself into a ball. Drawing the sheet over his head, he lowered his chin between his shoulders and rested it on his collarbone. His knees contracted until they nearly touched his stomach. All drawn together like that, he imagined himself a woodchuck burrowed deeply into a hole, retreating from the open world of danger. He felt miserable. Thoughts of a courtroom with a judge and witnesses and the whole town gathered to glare at him made his closed eyes burn. He sought refuge again in his fantasy of being an animal safe in its hole. With one paw he would pull some grass across the opening so no one could know he was there. Owlie sank into a troubled sleep full of vivid dreams. A big round face was coming at him and growing bigger and bigger. He tried to wake up but felt weighted and dragged back into the depths of sleep.

At last with a struggle he forced himself to open his eyes and saw the morning light pouring through his bedroom window.

Knowing he must face the day, he got stiffly out of bed and walked over to the window. A brazen sun was shining on a calm sea. The day would be a scorcher. For the first time the thought of his paper route filled him with distaste. He wondered whether to leave a paper at the house of the surly man and decided that as he was owed for nearly a week, he'd finish out the remaining days and then collect. Besides, he hadn't exactly been fired.

At breakfast he tried to make a little show of cheerfulness for his mother's sake, then went out to the stable and saddled up. Mystery had never been whisked around the paper route at such a clip before. On every soft bit of ground he was pressed into a canter, and Owlie tossed papers onto porches like rockets, not stopping to talk to anyone. His whole thought was to get away from the village, away from people, and have a swim.

He was trotting down the lane toward home when he noticed a group of people collected in front of the Dovers' house.

"Oh, Owlie!" cried Mrs. Dover, running out to him. "Bud's dying!" Her eyes were red and tears were rolling down her fat cheeks.

"Dying!" said Owlie aghast. He pulled Mystery to a stop, and Sam flopped down in the dusty road, panting and glad of a rest.

"What's the matter with him?" he asked, feeling awkward as he looked at the woman's distraught face.

But Mrs. Dover had burst into loud howls of grief. Mrs. Bladen and Mrs. Wilson, assisted by the grocer's wife, were holding up Mrs. Dover so she wouldn't collapse entirely, and between them they managed to explain.

It appeared that the night before, Bud had gone to a party at Beachport and around ten o'clock had consumed a big plate of creamed chicken, as had all the other guests. Unfortunately the creamed chicken, instead of being left in the refrigerator, had been sitting out all day in the heat, and everyone who had eaten any of it had become violently ill a few hours later. In fact the doctor in Beachport was so busy working on the people there that he hadn't yet arrived to help Bud.

"He's dying; he really is!" moaned Mrs. Dover.

Owlie stared at her, wondering why anyone could get so worked up even if Bud were to die. But he supposed mothers were funny that way.

"It's a terrible thing not having a doctor in the

village anymore," said Mrs. Bladen. "You never know when a sudden emergency will arise."

"Oh, dear! Oh, dear! Oh, dear!" cried Mrs. Dover hysterically. "If I could only see a doctor walk up the path this minute, I'd pray the holy angels to bless him all the rest of his life. My poor boy has thrown up forty-two times if he has once; there's nothing left inside him at all. He's as weak as a newborn kitten. Truly I can't watch him for another minute. His father's with him now."

"Mrs. Dover," said Owlie in a loud voice. "If you will please be quiet a minute I will tell you something. And the rest of you too," he added. "Listen, I might be able to get you a doctor if Bud's really as sick as you say."

"Oh, he is, he is!" cried Mrs. Dover. "Isn't he?" she asked the others.

Their solemn faces seemed to confirm Mrs. Dover's words, so Owlie went on. "I don't know whether I can do anything but I might. Dr. Delafield's out on the island. His face is terribly hurt. He doesn't want to see people because he looks awful. Would you promise, would you swear, that none of you would stare or act scared if you saw him? He might come if Bud's really bad."

"I'd stare with my eyes full of joy if I could

see dear Dr. Delafield, no matter what shape he's in!" cried Mrs. Dover. "Oh, Owlie, try to make him come. Beg him to come. Please, Owlie."

"I'll try," said Owlie briefly. He dropped on the ground the bag in which he carried his papers. Dismounting, he started unfastening the girth of his saddle.

"May I leave this here on your fence?" he asked. "We'll ride bareback together if he'll come."

"Aren't you going in a boat?" asked the grocer's wife. "Surely you don't mean you're going to the island on a horse!"

"Yes, I am," said Owlie.

"May all blessings be on you, Owlie. My, but it's a brave boy he is to ride straight into the water!" cried Mrs. Dover, turning toward the grocer's wife.

Would he come? Owlie wondered. Would he come in daylight when people were sure to see him? It had been different before when Owlie had persuaded him to come to his mother's help. The dawn had only been breaking, and no one was up yet.

The horse by now knew the route, and he followed the sand bar with very little guidance from the boy. "You love it over there, don't you?" said Owlie, patting his neck as they splashed toward the rocks and pine trees, all the while keeping in line with the no-trespassing sign on the strip of sand. "You like your jumping lessons and you like running loose on an island. Maybe you think this is where you belong. Mystery of Hideaway Island. That's what I'll have them put on the program when you get to be a famous jumping horse. We'll win first prize together, and they'll put your name on a big silver cup. That is, if you still belong to me," he said under his breath. He imagined policemen marching up to take Mystery away and give him to Mr. Hammond, and he shuddered as if the hot day made him feel cold.

Dr. Delafield was fishing from the rocks. He had just landed a big flounder as Owlie trotted his horse ashore.

"Hi," said Owlie. "Someone's awfully sick. He needs a doctor."

"Who is it?" asked Dr. Delafield, who was carefully removing the hook from the mouth of his flapping fish.

"It's Bud. Mrs. Dover said please would you . . . would I beg you to come."

"What's the matter with him?" asked Dr. Delafield.

"He's dying," said Owlie.

"As bad as that?" said the doctor. "While there's life there's hope. Isn't that the boy who is your enemy?"

"Yes, but his mother doesn't want him to die."

"My bag's over here now," said the doctor briefly. "I'll get it." He laid the fish in the shade under some ferns and walked toward the shack.

As before, they mounted in turn while Mystery stood without moving. Dr. Delafield shoved half an apple into Owlie's hand. "Here's his reward," he said.

The boy stretched his hand forward beside the horse's neck and saw his head turn, then felt the apple being taken from his fingers. The doctor put an arm around Owlie's waist, and they started off.

"The girl I pulled out of that fire was one of my patients," he said. "I had operated on her a couple of days before to take out her appendix. She told me she used to live around this part of the country and that she had had to leave behind a horse she loved. She picked apples from his back and always gave him a piece as a reward for standing still."

They had reached the water and were starting the trip back. "Mystery, it was you," said Owlie. "I'll bet it was you."

"I'll bet it was too," said the doctor. "I hear from

186

her sometimes. I'm going to tell her that her horse has found a good home."

"What's the trouble with this boy?" asked the doctor as they reached the shore in front of Westerly. His voice sounded irritable. Owlie guessed he dreaded the idea of meeting people. "If it's not a serious emergency, you know I don't want to go."

"Yes, I know," said Owlie, "but it is. I think he's terribly sick. He throws up all the time."

The little group was still standing in front of the Dovers' house. Owlie's saddle was still resting on the fence.

Now we will see, thought Owlie. Will they or won't they behave right?

To his relief he saw the grocer's wife and Mrs. Bladen step forward, smiling as if they had rehearsed a scene. "Welcome back, doctor," they said almost with one voice, and then they both looked away with studied casualness to watch some gulls that were flying by.

But Mrs. Dover, her whole thought on her son, cried out unaffectedly. "Bless you, bless you. Come this way. I know now my Bud will get well."

SIXTEEN

Half an hour later the doctor opened the door and beckoned Owlie to come inside. Wanting to find someone who could take care of his horse, the boy looked at the little group of sympathetic neighbors, who were still standing about, and noticed Roy.

"Will you hold Mystery?" asked Owlie. "You can let him eat grass. Just see that he doesn't step on the reins."

Roy gave Owlie an apprehensive look and took over the horse in a gingerly fashion.

"He'll be all right," said Owlie encouragingly.

Roy was carefully not looking at Dr. Delafield. "Wow, he certainly got messed up!" he said softly to Owlie. "You wouldn't recognize him."

"His eyes look at you the same as before," said Owlie.

"If he's got the guts to go around looking like that, we mustn't stare at him," said Roy.

"After a little while you don't want to stare," said Owlie. "It's just him. You forget his face."

"Bud's better," said the doctor, ushering Owlie through the door. "You were right. It was a very near thing. He should rest now. I've given him a hypodermic and sent for the equipment to give him a saline drip; he's dehydrated from throwing up. Before he goes off to sleep he has something he wants to say to you."

Mr. and Mrs. Dover were standing beside Bud's bed. The mother's plump cheeks were still teary and the father seemed to have lost for the moment his swaggering, aggressive attitude. His shoulders were slumped and his usually red face was pale.

Stretched on a rumpled sheet, Bud's hulking form had the weak and exhausted appearance of someone very ill. There was an unpleasant odor in the room.

Dr. Delafield took Owlie's arm and led him close to the bed.

In a gesture of greeting, Bud raised a languid hand an inch or two from his chest, where it was lying. When he spoke his voice sounded so faint that Owlie could scarcely hear the words.

"I told them I did it. It wasn't you. I threw the stone." His eyes closed suddenly and the doctor touched Owlie's arm. Together they tiptoed quietly out, followed by Mr. and Mrs. Dover.

In the scarred and twisted face, Dr. Delafield's eyes were kind. "Confession is good for the soul," he said. "Now he'll sleep quietly."

Mr. Dover's black eyebrows were working convulsively. "I'm sorry, Owlie," he said. "It was what they call circumstantial evidence. I saw you alone there with that stone, and I jumped to conclusions."

Mrs. Dover's easy tears were flowing again. "The doctor has made us see that you can kill a person's reputation by bearing false witness. We've promised to tell Mr. Hammond and all the other people we spoke to that it wasn't you."

"I hope Bud can get his car," said Owlie uncomfortably.

"We can't be angry with him now. We came too near losing him," said Mr. Dover. His thick eyebrows met over his nose in a puzzled frown. "Why did you get help for Bud?" he asked.

"If you're a doctor you have to help people," said Owlie simply.

"But you're not a doctor."

"I'm going to be," said Owlie. He paused. "If I can make it," he added.

"Here comes the man from Beachport bringing the saline-drip equipment," said Dr. Delafield, looking out the window. "Owlie, I'll meet you at Westerly later. Mr. Dover will drive me up. Would you give me a ride back this afternoon before the tide gets too high?"

"Sure," said Owlie. "If you want to go later Dad could row you across."

"No," said the doctor. "I don't want to stay too long."

Mrs. Dover pressed a glass of milk and a piece of cake into Owlie's hands before she would let him go. "Take it; please do. You must be hungry. Bygones are bygones, I hope?" she questioned, her tears beginning to drip again.

She's like a faucet, thought Owlie. "Oh, sure," he said awkwardly as he took the food she thrust upon him. The cake was stale but the milk tasted good, for he was thirsty.

When he went to get his horse he found Mr. Dover standing outside talking to Roy.

"I told him—" said the man gruffly, "I told him to tell the other fellows it wasn't you." With a jerk of his head he turned and walked away.

Owlie hated to be the center of this uncomfortable situation. He felt highly embarrassed as he took the reins from Roy. "Thanks for holding him," he said.

"Hey, I guess Bud's sure being taken over the bumps this week," said Roy. "First he cuts his hand on a broken bottle, then he eats some rotten chicken, and now he's got his old man after him."

Owlie was putting on his saddle and fastening the girth. He grinned. "So long," he said, and mounted Mystery.

Somehow he didn't feel like going right home. What he felt like doing was jumping off some energy. There was great happiness in him that he needed to express. But where could he find jumps? Why, of course. The breakwaters out on the ocean side beyond the point!

When they reached the lighthouse, Sam sat down on the grass and pretended to be very interested in the lighthouse keeper's cat. Owlie guessed he was tired and would wait for them right there.

The breakwaters, exposed by a low tide, lay like a series of walls running from the water up to the dry sand.

"Come on, Mystery, let's jump," said Owlie. His throat tightened and his blood tingled, for the walls were high and solid and allowed for no mistakes.

Setting his horse into a measured canter, he headed toward the first barrier. He felt the power under him, saw the working of shoulder muscles, felt the onward drive communicated from the bit to the reins in his hand.

He leaned forward on his horse's neck and experienced a lift and upsurge as Mystery took off, then the flight through the air as they cleared the wall, and after that the thud of landing as the horse's hoofs struck on wet sand.

They cantered away and the next jump loomed up. Owlie's heart was singing a song of happiness, of confidence in his horse, and of exultation at being part of this great energy that could spurn the earth and fly through the air. It was as if the strong legs were his own, for he and his horse were one indissoluble unit. He was providing the brains and the persuasion, and the horse, the power. They were one.

As they cleared the last barrier, Owlie laid his cheek on his horse's mane and said, "Mystery," in a voice filled with joy.

Jogging toward home, relaxed and at peace, he began to comprehend that Bud probably wouldn't bother him anymore. Of course Bud wouldn't like him—Owlie was bright enough to realize that you

usually didn't like people you had wronged—but he was pretty certain that no longer would he have to endure Bud's teasing and tripping and mockery on the way from the school bus.

Something made him want to go home by way of the village, for now he felt once again like sitting straight and riding confidently. Everyone was going to know, if they didn't already, that this was his horse, honestly purchased with forty dollars that he had earned himself.

Several people greeted him when he started to ride past the post office. He guessed Roy had been talking, because there was a special tone in the voices that spoke to him, and he saw Roy inside, taking his mail out of his box.

"Glad to see you, Owlie," someone called.

"Your horse is a beauty. You take good care of him," declared the surly little man who was Owlie's customer. He had an ashamed look as he made the remark.

Just then Roy came out, carrying a couple of letters, and sudden inspiration flashed into Owlie's mind. He beckoned Roy to approach and spoke eagerly. "You know," he said, "Dr. Delafield's up at Westerly right now. If people called on him and asked him to be the doctor here, maybe he'd live at Westerly this winter."

"Hey, that would be great," said Roy. "But they couldn't stare at him. If they stared we'd fix 'em, wouldn't we?"

"You bet," said Owlie. "We sure would."

Both boys knew that the people standing about had heard their remarks. And there was something else they knew. Anything of interest said in a village travels by grapevine from one end to the other within an hour.

"I'll do something about this," said Roy, giving a conspiratorial wink.

Owlie waved his hand in affirmation and pressed Mystery with his legs to get going. Presently the sound of his horse's clattering hoofs faded from the main street as he turned off onto a side road.

It seemed to him a good idea to go up to Westerly. His instinct told him a lot would be happening up there within the next hour, and he wanted to be on hand to prepare the doctor for visitors.

Inside the gates, near the drive of crushed clamshells, his father was trimming the faded heads from flowers to keep the plants blossoming at their best. He looked up at the sound of the horse's hoof beats and smiled at Owlie.

"Sam looks hot," he said.

The big dog's sides were heaving under his black

fur coat, and from his wide-open mouth his pink tongue lolled and dripped moisture. With a grateful grunt the dog flopped down in the shade of a tree while his saliva continued to drip on the green grass.

"He's pretty smart now about taking shortcuts or waiting for me and not going the whole way if he's tired," said Owlie.

"It's unusually hot today," remarked his father. "Let's see." He looked at his watch. "It's about lunchtime and he can swim and cool off in front of our house."

"I'm not coming home to lunch," said Owlie.

"Why not?" asked his father, surprised.

"Look, Dad, I think Roy Bladen's going to sort of organize people to come up here and try to get Dr. Delafield to be our doctor in the village. People just have to get used to his face and then everything will be okay, but he thinks he'd upset his patients. He thinks they would be sick enough already without being made sicker by seeing him or something. Roy and I want to show him that's not so."

His father nodded slowly. "Good idea," he said. "I'll go home and get your mother. We'd like to be in on this too."

Owlie walked Mystery up and down the drive a few times to cool him off, then tied him to a rail fence in the shade of a tree near Sam. He always carried a lead rope and halter in the bottom of his bag in case he had to tie his horse while delivering papers, and now these had come in handy.

When he knocked on the side door at Westerly the doctor, who apparently had been watching him through the window, opened the door without surprise.

"Glad to see you, but aren't you a little early? I don't need a taxi back to the island for another hour or two."

"Well, I . . . at least . . . I thought . . . maybe we should put the flag up," said Owlie with sudden inspiration. "You're in residence so . . . well . . . you used to, when you were here, always put up the flag."

The doctor looked at him keenly. "What about a little lunch first. I see your horse is grazing on the edge of the lawn. Don't you want to take him a bucket of water and give Sam a drink too?"

"Sure," said Owlie, "that would be a good idea."

"We'll eat in the kitchen," said the doctor. "You'll find a bucket in the garage."

When Owlie returned from watering his animals

he found the doctor opening a tin of sardines and a box of crackers he had found on a shelf. They sat down at the kitchen table.

The boy kept peering out the window as he ate and finally the doctor inquired rather sharply, "What are you looking for, Owlie?"

"Oh . . . ah, that is . . . there were some birds," said Owlie lamely.

"I've been thinking about what you said about wanting to be a doctor," said the man. "You know, Owlie, if you really want to go to college you will be able to, if you continue to get good marks in school. There are scholarships people can get. Once I lent some money to a boy who was really serious about going to medical school. I knew he would pay me back when he began earning and he did. I believe in you, Owlie. I'll stand in back of you if you continue on in the way you seem to be going. Doctors are needed. There aren't enough of them."

"That's *so*, Dr. Delafield!" cried Owlie eagerly. "Doctors *are* needed. Hey, what about the flag? Couldn't we put it up?"

"If you want to," said the man, giving Owlie a puzzled look. "Come on. I keep it in a box in the front hall."

They hitched the flag to the rope on the flagpole

and hauled away together until the Stars and Stripes waved proudly above their heads.

"We'd better go inside," said Owlie suddenly. He had seen some cars heading toward the Westerly driveway.

The doctor looked at the boy curiously but followed him back into the hallway of the house.

"What's going on here?" asked the doctor. "You're acting awfully peculiar."

Owlie's motive had been to get the doctor out of the strong sunshine so that the red welts, the misshapen jaw, and the drawn mouth would be less glaringly revealed. He shut the door behind them and looked out the window.

"I think someone's come to see you. They must have noticed the flag and decided you were in residence," said Owlie solemnly.

His guile was not subtle enough to fool the doctor, who gave the boy a sharp look as he said, "They could hardly have arrived that quickly."

A knock on the door announced the first of the visitors.

"Go and find out who that is," said the doctor.

Owlie pulled open the big front door and saw his parents. His mother was carrying a basket covered with a clean napkin. "My wife wants to say, sir, that she has made you an apple pie to take back to the island," said Thomas Jennings.

"Thank you. That was very thoughtful," said the doctor. "Ask how her shoulder feels nowadays," he instructed Owlie.

The boy spelled the message rapidly on his fingers.

His mother smiled, then quickly spelled a few words.

"She says it feels fine," Owlie interpreted.

"We all wish, sir, that you could stay here at Westerly this winter," said Owlie's father. "The village needs a doctor, and we would certainly be honored to have you."

"It's nice of you to say that," said Dr. Delafield.

"There are some other people outside who would like to have a word with you too," continued Owlie's father. "May we let them in?"

The doctor winced as if something pained him and put a hand to his face. "All right," he said, "show them in."

Owlie jumped to open the door and a long file slowly entered led by Roy, who was followed by Mr. and Mrs. Dover; then the mother of the little girl named Rosie, whom Sam had accidentally knocked over on the beach; then the grocer's wife;

next the mailman; after that Dr. Little, the vet, followed by Mr. and Mrs. Bladen; then Mrs. Wilson and her son, Red; and so on until perhaps fifty people had passed through the room and had shaken the doctor's hand warmly. All his visitors were saying more or less the same thing: "Dr. Delafield, we need you."

As the last person filed out, the door was suddenly pushed open again and Rosie, who had been left outside, came bouncing in. Her pigtails were tied with red ribbons, which stuck out in a saucy manner, and she was dragging a rag doll by one leg.

"Rosie, come back here this minute!" cried her mother anxiously from outside.

But Rosie was not minding. Seeing Dr. Delafield, she walked slowly and solemnly up to him and stopped by his side.

"You have a funny face," she said.

Owlie gasped and glared at her, but the doctor fixed his kind eyes on the child. "Yes, I do," he said quietly.

"But I like you," said Rosie and turning, she dragged her doll behind her out of the house.

Dr. Delafield smiled and looked at Owlie. "I seem to be wanted. I think I'll stay. You hatched a little plot here, didn't you? People seemed to bear up better than I would have expected."

The boy took a limping step toward him and pushing his glasses up on his nose he said, "It was you who told me it didn't matter how a person looked; you said it was what was inside him that counted."

"So I did," said the doctor. "Listen, Owlie, why don't you buy some glasses that fit? I've got a job for you after school this autumn helping me file medical papers, and you can earn some extra money if you'd like to. There are several other things you can help me with also. I imagine you're going to need money to buy feed for your horse this winter."

"I've been kind of worried about that," said Owlie, "but I don't want you to pay me—you gave me all those jumping lessons and everything."

"You've done a thing or two for me, Owlie. You're not in my debt. I need you to work for me —and you need a job. What do you say?"

Owlie swallowed and nodded his head vigorously. "That will be great. Thanks a lot, Dr. Delafield."

"Are you all set to ride me over to the island in about a half hour? I have one or two things to do here, and then I'll be ready to go."

"Anytime," said Owlie. "I'll just have a look at Mystery and Sam and see that they're all right."

The doctor nodded and turned toward a desk in an adjoining room.

Owlie stepped outside, letting the screen door bang behind him. He looked back quickly and wondered whether to say he was sorry, but the doctor had disappeared.

Sam still lay under the tree. Near the fence Mystery was cropping short grass with quick wrenching bites. Owlie noticed he had forgotten to run the stirrup irons up the leathers when he had dismounted. And the girth should have been loosened to give his horse a breather. He was busily rectifying his omissions when he heard behind him steps crunching on the driveway, and he looked over his shoulder after quickly easing the girth by a couple of holes. Roy Bladen was walking toward him with an anxious expression on his face. "Is he going to stay?" he asked. "I could have murdered that little kid Rosie."

"That was all right," Owlie answered. "He didn't seem to mind. It kind of seemed to help somehow. Yes, he's going to stay. Once he told me he had always wanted to live at Westerly, so maybe he's glad."

"Hey, how about going swimming?" asked Roy. "Red and I thought we'd go along about three o'clock."

"Sure, I guess so," said Owlie. "I've got to take the doctor back first."

"We'll stop by for you on our way," said Roy.

"Okay," Owlie agreed. It was hard to sound casual—he wanted to give a big grin, he wanted to jump, he wanted to shout. But not until Roy had disappeared through the gate did he make a move. Then he gave Mystery a hearty smack on the neck and jumped up as high as he could to grab at a tree branch while Sam, catching his elation, barked and wagged his tail.

"Hey," cried Owlie, throwing into the air the leaves he had torn away, "we'll have to hurry home from the island! I don't want to be late for swimming."

HARPER TROPHY BOOKS
you will enjoy reading

The Little House Books *by Laura Ingalls Wilder*

HARPER & ROW, PUBLISHERS, INC.
10 East 53rd Street, New York, N.Y. 10022